J

500006989522

SJ

GW01464992

Way of the Hunted

Way of the Hunted

LEE YOUNGER

A Black Horse Western

ROBERT HALE · LONDON

Photoset in North Wales by
Derek Doyle & Associates, Mold, Flintshire.
Printed and bound in Great Britain by
WBC Book Manufacturers Limited, Bridgend.

For Chris and Glyn
Missed By All Who Knew You

One

I watched them coming from a long way off, five men, strangers. Leastways, I didn't recognise the horses, and that was the first thing I noticed about anyone – the animal they rode, and its condition. Horses are more interesting than people, mostly more intelligent too. Whoever these men were, they were moving with purpose and heading straight for my farm. Even from a distance, before making out any faces, I knew these were men that I wouldn't like.

Wasn't much I could do about it though. Only weapon I had in the house was an old single-shot carbine. I had never found out if it was the rifle that couldn't shoot straight, or me. Whatever these men had in mind they were going to be disappointed. There was nothing in the house worth stealing. Not much outside either. I had been fighting a losing battle against the land for most of my life. Never even had a crop worth speaking of. Most of my soil disappeared into the next county every time the wind blew.

The land had beaten me and it was time I accepted that fact. Trouble was, once I accepted that fact I had but one course to follow, and Ma wouldn't like that. I glanced at her grave up there on the knoll, feeling the shame and guilt eating away at me again. But I had made my vow a long time ago and would have to see it through.

My first impression had been right as the men came to a halt. The leader, a heavy-set man with mean eyes, looked at me for a long while before speaking.

'This Jeff Wilde's place, boy?'

'Was once,' I said, offering no further information. These men were hunters, and Jefferson Wilde was the quarry. Hardly surprising, considering his reputation. Still it was the first time anyone had ever come here looking for him. It was a long time since anyone had laid eyes on him and most of the talk about him was spoken in whispers. Those whispers grew silent when I came into sight.

'Where is he, boy?'

I shrugged. 'Who knows? He hasn't been near this place for years. If he had I'd be leading you to his bones right now.'

The man grinned broadly. 'That's pretty big talk for a boy. Take a look around, Kelly. Don't miss anything.'

One of his men dismounted and limped towards the house. I didn't mind. Another of his mind dismounted to check the barn. There was caution in their every movement. Couldn't blame them any. From what I knew of Jeff Wilde, he was a hard man to tangle with.

Kelly, the man with the limp, was first to return. 'No sign of him ever being here, Kelp. Looks like the kid lives alone.'

The leader nodded. 'Kelly there is still carrying a bullet with the compliments of Wilde. Let us know if you hear of him. Kelly'd take it kind of personal if someone got to him first.'

My blood was heating up. Talk of Jefferson Wilde always affected me that way, and I'd never had sense enough to put a curb on my tongue. 'You're way down the line, mister. My grievance goes back twelve, fourteen years. That gives me prior claim on his life.'

Kelp laughed out loud. A nineteen-year-old kid was sounding off about killing Jeff Wilde. 'If talk could do it, boy, you'd sure be in with a chance, but Jeff Wilde isn't an easy man to kill. A lot of men could testify to that – if they were still around. Tell you what I'll do: when we catch up with him we'll tell him all about you. At least he'll die with a smile on his lips that way. Got a name we can frighten him with?'

'Wilde,' I told him quietly, 'Jim Wilde.'

I watched the men ride away before heading for the knoll. The tracks were there, as I had known they would be. About four days back, I had found tracks and used cigarette butts near the corral, as if the man, whoever he was, had stood there for quite a spell observing the house. I had tried to keep watch and find out who it was, but after two nights, fatigue had gotten the better of me. The thought of someone spying on me that way sent a cold chill down my spine.

Telling myself that the man meant me no harm was of little consolation. I was alone in the house with only a single-shot rifle for protection. Killing me would have been the easiest thing in the world for him, if that was what he had in mind. Maybe the time wasn't yet right. Still, he had him a reason for being here and I didn't know what that reason was.

The wooden marker wasn't much, but it was the best I was capable of. Ma deserved a lot better. I touched the rough-hewn wood in apology. Ma wouldn't like what I had in mind, but each man had to have a purpose in life. I had no choice. I had to reach Jefferson Wilde before Kelp and his bunch did. His life belonged to me. It wouldn't be easy, but

I knew something that Kelp didn't. Jefferson Wilde had done a lot of travelling before meeting Ma and settling down, allbeit for a short time.

On the rare occasions Ma had talked about Jeff Wilde she mentioned a dream they had shared of settling down in a place called Mustang Valley in Oregon. I was betting that Jefferson Wilde was already settled there with no thought of his past life or the wife and son he had left behind to struggle against a dry-dirt farm. Ma's fight had ended four years ago. Mine ended today. The land had beaten me, just as I had always known it would.

Come morning, I would head into town and take up the offer Mr Crawley had made me on the farm. I hated the thought of leaving Ma behind, but I would always carry her memory with me, and the Crawleys would tend her grave for me. The guilt of what I had to do would stay with me, too, for the rest of my life.

There were no fresh footprints on the knoll or near the corral when I took my usual walk around the next morning. Looked like the man, whoever he was, had decided to move on again. It had been that way for quite a few years now. All of a sudden the tracks appeared for a week or so, then nothing. I hadn't made no sense of it. The man was still in my thoughts as I saddled Peg and headed for town.

11

I had never been one to accept defeat easily, but it would have taken a lot of money for irrigation and such if the farm was ever to amount to much. Mr Crawley, the storekeeper, was the only man around here with money enough to make the land pay. Being a storekeeper was an easier life but, I guess, Mr Crawley was a frustrated farmer at heart. And my farm was the one he had set his heart on. He could have taken the farm off me by letting me get way over my head in debt at the store, but that wasn't his way. The price he had offered was a good one; only stubbornness had kept me from accepting it before.

The usual benign smile wasn't on his face as I entered his store. I soon found out why.

'There are five men in town asking about your father, Jim. It looks as if they intend staying around here for a while. It could mean trouble for you.'

'We've already met,' I told him. 'They called at the farm last night, helped make my decision for me. The farm's yours, if you still want it.'

The farm had been his dream for a long time but his main concern was for me. 'If you are sure that's the way you want it, Jim.'

'It's the way it has to be. There are some things I'll be needing. I'm heading out tonight.'

'I'll have everything ready for you. You'll need a good horse under you. Simmons has a sorrel for sale, if you're interested.'

I knew the horse he spoke of. I had busted him, but it had been a close-run thing. Some of my muscles still ached at the memory, but if that horse was now for sale, I wanted it. Crawley would make the deal later when Simmons came in. I nodded acceptance as one of Kelp's men came into the store; it was the man with the stiff leg.

It seemed like Mr Crawley was starting to enjoy our conspiracy. 'I'm sorry, Jim,' he said loudly. 'I can't extend you any more credit. Times are hard all over. Perhaps it's time you gave up the farm, got yourself a job. At least, you'd have some cash in your pockets then. Just you and a worn-out horse, no one can run a farm that way.'

His plan worked. Satisfied that I wouldn't be going far on an ageing horse and with no money in my jeans, the man with the bad leg walked out.

I grinned. 'Almost had me feeling sorry for myself then, Mr Crawley. Remind me never to play poker with you.'

'You won't get the chance, Jim.' I gave him my piece of paper. 'Everything you need on this list, Jim?'

'Everything except a new saddle, rifle and pistol. I may have missed a few other things if you think of them.'

He didn't like the idea of me carrying guns but knew I would have need of them.

'I'll be waiting here for you tonight, Jim. Everything will be ready.' He hesitated. 'I never knew your father, Jim, but knowing your mother I'd say she saw things in him that few others wanted to see. Look for those things, son.'

I wasn't about to get into a discussion about Jefferson Wilde and destroy Mr Crawley's faith in his fellow beings.

'Take whatever I owe you out of the farm money, Mr Crawley. I don't reckon I'll have too much time to hang around when I come back.'

He nodded. 'It will all be settled. The sorrel will be out back ready. I won't ask where you're heading. That way I won't be lying if those men come in here asking questions.'

'They won't be coming round here, Mr Crawley,' I said quietly. 'As soon as they find out that I've left they'll be coming along right behind me.'

TWO

One of Kelp's men was out there watching the house as I stepped out into the lengthening shadows and headed for the barn. The need for a smoke had betrayed the watcher's presence in the tangle brush an hour before. For some reason, Kelp believed that Jefferson Wilde was headed back this way, but he was as wrong as a man could get. If Jeff Wilde ever had a reason for coming back here, she was now buried on the knoll.

My plans were already made as I fed Peg. I hated the thought of having to say goodbye to her, but I would have need of a younger horse beneath me if I was to get away from Kelp and his men. Still, Peg would have herself a good home, and a life of luxury compared to what she had had here on the farm. Mrs Drake had a soft spot for Peg, never failing to greet her with an apple or a sugar lump whenever we passed her home on the outskirts of town. She would be the proudest woman in town with Peg between the shafts of that old buggy of hers. Mrs Drake's own horse had died a couple of years back and she'd never had money enough to replace her. They would be good for each other.

For some reason, Jefferson had set a back door into the barn he had built before I was born. Maybe he had wanted some kind of escape route even way back then. I checked that door now, not wanting any creaking to betray me when I made my move. It opened easier than I expected. Satisfied, I headed back to the house.

It was almost completely dark when I finished cooking my supper. At the moment I had no real taste for food but there was no way of knowing when I would have time enough for my next meal. As soon as Kelp found out I was missing he'd be hot on my tail.

I ate quickly, giving the taste no time to settle on my tongue. With my kind of cooking it was the best way. Most of the kerosene had been emptied out of the lamp before I lit it. With luck, that lamp would burn for an hour or so after I had left – making it look like I'd extinguished it and gone to bed. That was the plan, anyhow – the only one I had.

The moon was on my side, hiding its face behind dark clouds as I slipped out of a back

16

window and crawled to the barn. Ten minutes later I was in the saddle and heading towards town, keeping the barn between me and the watcher until I reached the dip and followed it to town. There would be no riding the main trail tonight. Kelp was probably smart enough to have another man watching the approach to town; it wasn't a chance I could afford to take. If he caught me now there would be hell to pay. The fact that I was only following a hunch wouldn't satisfy him, and he wasn't about to take the chance of me getting to Jefferson Wilde first and warning him.

Mr Crawley was as good as his word. The sorrel was already saddled and waiting for me out back of the store. I re-acquainted myself with the sorrel before tapping quietly on the back door of the store. It opened quickly and I was ushered inside. Everything was ready for me. I had never owned so much in my life before. I had a couple of new shirts, jeans and a selection of new hats to choose from. A grey wide-brimmed J.B. Stetson fitted proudly on my head. The shabby remains of my own headgear was tossed aside.

I dressed quickly in my new clothes in a curtained-off alcove that Mr Crawley had set into his store, and I felt like king of the hill. Mr Crawley had a new Winchester and a .45 Colt Peacemaker waiting for me when I came out, both weapons loaded. I had never used a short gun in my life before but trouble would soon be dogging my trail. Learning to use the Colt would have to be my prime consideration.

Leaving Peg in Mrs Drake's little stable had been the toughest part of things so far. She had been a part of my life for a long time. As soon as she heard Mrs Drake's voice come morning she would whinny a greeting, and get herself found. I had wanted to leave a note explaining things but hadn't been able to find the words. I asked Mr Crawley if he would do it for me.

He nodded. 'That man Kelp is in the saloon with three of his friends. I don't know where the other man is, so be careful. I wish there was some other way, Jim.'

So did I. Just the thought of all that country out there scared the hell out of me. Life had been hard here but there were a lot of good people ready to come to my aid if ever I had need of it. Only pride had kept me from asking for help, but it was always there on offer. Out there, I would be more alone than I had ever been in my life.

'I know what you've got in mind, Jim, and there's no need for me to tell you how I feel about it. You are going to have to live with it afterwards, and I don't think you'll be able to do that. I never knew Jefferson Wilde. He had gone before I came here, and a man doesn't vanish without a reason.

18

From what I've heard, he's a hard man to cross and very useful with a gun. It might be better if you just shook Kelp off your trail and disappeared like he did. Find yourself a place to settle down and build a new life.'

There was sense in what he said, but the hate had been burning inside me for too long for me to see reason. I had more money than I had ever seen in my life, but I was going to use that money to hunt down and kill a man.

The sun had long since risen and gone away again to visit another part of the world before I reined the sorrel in and checked my back trail, the hunger aching inside me. Satisfied that I had lost Kelp and his men, I unsaddled the sorrel and set to making a small fire for coffee and a quick meal. Every bone in my body and the muscles on my sit-me-down were numb. I had spent close on eighteen hours in the saddle. It was something I would have to get used to. I had a long journey ahead of me.

Even the smell of my cooking couldn't take the edge off my appetite as I sliced bacon into the pan, but there was a lost, empty feeling inside me. Everything I had ever known was back in my past now. I was a stranger in a raw savage land. The land had become my enemy now, more real than Kelp and his men. For the first time I realized that I didn't have knowledge enough to survive in country such as this. It was a merciless endless land. Just the vast emptiness of the country was enough to frighten me.

It seemed like there was nothing ahead of me, but there could be no turning back. By now Kelp has discovered that I was missing and would be hot on my trail. There hadn't been time enough for me to cover up my tracks. My only thought had been to get as much distance between Kelp and me and to keep it that way. It was a mistake that could have proved fatal.

'Hope you've got some of that grub and coffee to spare.'

The voice startled me and I turned quickly, my hand dipping for my gun.

'Don't do it, boy. You won't make it and I'd sure hate to shoot you.'

I let my hand rest on my gunbutt as my eyes rested on the stranger. I didn't recognize him as one of Kelp's men, but he could have had others that I didn't know about. He might have been using this man to get me off guard. 'What makes you think you could beat me, mister?'

'That's a new gun on your hip, boy. Doubt if you've had it more than a couple of days – not even time enough to learn how to use it. Everything about you is new, boy: hat, clothes, saddle, Winchester. Even using what you got under that hat of yours is new to you. Doubt if

you'll survive long. You ain't even got sense
enough to use the country to your advantage.'

Those quick eyes and brain of his hadn't missed
much. If he had been a part of Kelp's outfit he
would have known most of those things already,
but he didn't look like the type of hardcase Kelp
had with him when he came to the farm.

'You seem to know a lot about me, mister. Too
much, I'm thinking.'

'Only know what I see, boy. I'm not part of that
gang on your trail, if that's what's bothering you.'

I felt a cold tremor run through my body. How
the hell could he know about Kelp? I asked him
outright who had told him.

'You did, boy. You're running scared. Can't say I
blame you much for that. If I had five men on my
tail I'd be running scared, too. I cut your trail
along about noon. I was kind of short on coffee and
grub so I decided to tag along, maybe scrounge a
little grub. Since I picked you up you've avoided
towns, farms, any place where there are people.
Had to be a reason for that, so I hung back a while
until I saw those men tracking you. You're making
it easy for them; left a trail a blind man could
follow.'

The fact that he knew so much irked me. He
was making me look and sound like a greenhorn.
But I knew what I was doing, and wanted him to
know it, too. 'I didn't try to cover my tracks,

21

mister. I've got me a good horse and a head start. That's all I need.'

He shook his head in sorrow. 'That ain't smart, boy. I saw Kelp and his men cut off your trail. By now, they've got fresh horses under them and they'll be heading this way fast. Only a day or two before they run you down, unless you get smart in a hurry, but I can't see that happening.'

That was something I hadn't considered. Sure the sorrel was a good horse but I had been pushing him pretty hard. Only a matter of time until it took its toll. Kelp could pick up fresh horses just about any place and push them to the limit. The sorrel was a runner, I knew that, but there wasn't a horse alive that could outrun a bullet. It was a sure bet that Kelp would be shooting at the sorrel and not me. I had information he needed.

The fact that the stranger was only pointing out things that I should have realized for myself only made me more riled.

'What do you suggest?' I snapped.

'Use the country. Keep to the low ground, change course once in a while. Confuse them; slow them down, cover your tracks. Right now you're making a beeline for wherever you are heading. Sooner or later, they are going to realize that and cut you off. They want you bad, boy, and Kelp isn't the type to give up easy.'

'You must have been pretty close to them, mister, if you could hear names.'

He shook his head again. 'I ain't that dumb, boy. Kelp and me have locked horns a time or two. I got close enough to recognize him. That's as close as I want to get. Now about that grub? I ain't eaten for a long time.'

He winced a little as the first taste of my cooking hit him, but made no comment on it. But it sure must have been a long time since he had eaten because he went back for seconds. 'The name's Cole Masters, in case you're wondering. Where you heading?'

I shrugged, still suspicious about the man calling himself Cole Masters. He had come out of nowhere and found me in the middle of nothing but emptiness. 'North, maybe. Montana, Oregon, the Dakotas. Ain't set my mind yet.'

'There's a lot of country between here and them places, kid. Ain't wise for anyone to try and make it on their own. Best thing to do would be to get yourself a wagon and hitch onto a train heading the same way. But judging by your cooking you're probably in more danger from that than anything you might find out there.'

Sad part was I couldn't argue with him. His eyes had a faraway look in them.

'Had me a yearning for a long time to head for the mountains again too, kid. They get into a man's blood. When a man stands upon the mountains he can touch the clouds. Funny thing is what I remember most is sitting by my camp-fire at night listening to the thunder of the wild horse herd as they come down the valley. A man can't forget a place like that.'

I felt my blood run cold. Jeff Wilde had always talked to Ma about a valley where the horses run free and wild. It had always been his dream to settle there. If it was the same valley Cole Masters talked of it would be the place I would find Jefferson Wilde. But, just maybe, Masters knew who I was and was leading me into a trap. It was a risk I would have to take.

'Hope your coffee is strong enough to wash away the taste of your cooking. By the way, why is Kelp hunting you?'

'He thinks I've got information that he has need of. Thinks I can tell him where to find Jefferson Wilde, but I've got need to get to him first.'

'Jeff Wilde, huh?' Cole mused. 'That makes sense. Kelp will never get a better chance to kill him if he catches up with him now, even if he don't know it. You've got a long way to go, kid, just to warn a man. Jeff Wilde will owe you a big vote of thanks, if you make it.'

'He won't be thanking me,' I said coldly. 'He'll be cussing me from the other side of Hell.'

He looked at me for a long time, reading the

naked anger in my face before shaking his head in regret. 'Hate is a heavy burden for any man to carry, let alone one not yet full-growed. After a while, it weighs a man down and robs him of his own life. What did Jefferson Wilde do to you that makes you hate him so much?'

'He's my father. That's reason enough.'

Three

Only pain showed in that suddenly tired face as he lifted the coffee mug to his lips, but it had nothing to do with my brew. Maybe my cooking wasn't up to much, but I was kind of proud of my coffee. He nodded his approval without looking at me.

'What do you know about Jefferson Wilde, boy?'

'The name is Jim,' I told him, getting tired of him calling me "boy" all the time. 'I only know what I want to know. I figure that's enough.'

'Yeah, that's usually the case, boy. The less you know about a man the easier it is to kill him. Sometimes a man has reason for doing things. Someone else gets hurt but he doesn't mean it to be that way. And sometimes that reason makes sense only to himself. He's the one that gets hurt most but the decision is made and there's no going back.'

'Sounds like you are trying to defend him,

mister. Why defend someone you don't even know? Who are you anyway?'

'Cole Masters, and you are wrong about me not knowing your pa. I knew him, knew a lot of men like him. The war left a lot of men scarred. After it ended, the South had nothing. Each of us did anything we could just to survive, and it didn't matter too much which side of the law we rode on. It was Yankee law anyway. The carpetbaggers moved in like carrion to pick our bones. It was fight back or die. Your pa was a fighter, but there wasn't much left to fight for.'

'He had Ma and me,' I cut in quickly. 'Maybe he didn't reckon us worth fighting for. What kind of man would run out on his own family?'

'That's a question you will have to ask him yourself, kid – if you've got the guts. I can take you to him, but it will be up to you to find him.'

I wondered what he meant by that. Cole Masters had a way of saying things that I would have to get used to if I was to ride with him. He had meanings of his own that I couldn't yet grasp.

'What's the catch, mister? One minute you are defending him. Next minute you're offering to take me to him. You know what's going to happen when I meet up with him. I'm going to kill him, just as sure as sunset.'

'Or he'll kill you, boy. There aren't too many men around who could match Jeff Wilde with a

28

gun; not many who wanted to try even. The catch is you've got the money to outfit a trip to Oregon; I ain't. Sure, it would be cheaper if you went it alone, but even if you made it you wouldn't set eyes on Jefferson Wilde. I doubt that you'd make it. You don't know enough. The Oregon trail is already littered with the bones of those who didn't make it. If you teamed up with me you'd have a chance. You'd learn a lot along the way, maybe even how to use that gun of yours.'

There were things he wasn't telling me. For some reason he wanted to meet up with Jeff Wilde, too. I looked at him for a long time trying to read that granite face of his, but I failed. If it was just my money he was after I would have been dead by now and he would have been gone.

'Seems to me there's more to it than that, Mr Masters . . . something you're not telling me.'

He met my gaze evenly. 'Yeah, you're right. I owe Jeff Wilde, too, but I guarantee that you'll get first chance at him. Good enough?'

There was a strange empty feeling in the pit of my stomach that I didn't like. I gulped coffee to try and rid myself of it, but it stayed with me. What the hell kind of man was Jefferson Wilde anyhow? In less than a couple of days I had already come across six men who wanted him dead, and I wasn't counting myself. How many more were out there just waiting for their chance at him?

Sure, I had heard snatches of talk about him, most of it drying up when folks saw me coming. But I had still learned enough to know that he had ridden with a pretty tough bunch of men in his youth. He had a big reputation with a gun, and had never learned how to back up to any man. Ma had said nothing about him when I was growing up. Maybe she hoped he would come back one day and I would learn for myself what kind of man he was; or maybe she knew that there was too much hate in me to listen.

For a long time after I had reached my teen years, folks had looked at me with suspicion in their eyes as if expecting me to turn out to be just like my old man. It had taken a long time for me to prove them wrong, but I had got a certain satisfaction out of doing it.

'Good enough,' I told Masters. I had no real choice anyway. Just one day on the trail had taught me that I didn't yet know enough to make it on my own. If Cole Masters hadn't come along there was a good chance that I would have woken up tomorrow morning and found Kelp and his men sitting around my camp-fire. If I had got the chance to wake up.

He nodded. 'We'll rest up here for an hour or so before moving out. Kelp is too close for my liking. We'll leave the fire burning to lead him right here and buy us a little more time. From here on, you'll do as I say, when I say. No arguments, and no questions. OK?'

I voiced my agreement, even though I didn't like it. Cole Masters was the kind of man who had crossed a lot of rivers and climbed many a mountain in his time. Hell, I had never even seen a mountain or anything fit to be called a river.

By sun-up we were well away from my camp and headed in a new direction. A lot of almost empty waste land stretched before us without a tree in sight. But Masters seemed to know exactly where we were going. I kept my eyes peeled. I was a stranger in an alien land, not knowing what to expect. Even so I would have missed the sod-built trading post if Masters hadn't been along to lead me to it.

I had never seen such a place before, and I didn't like the feel of it as we stepped inside. A few oil lamps did little to brighten the place or relieve the dankness of it. The three occupants of the place stopped playing cards long enough to look at us as we entered, recognizing me for what I was, a greenhorn with the smell of a dirt farm still with him. Maybe the smell of money was with me, too.

Money seemed to be the one thing they were short of as a big bearded man pushed his stack of matches into the game and called. He won but only had himself a bigger stack of matches to show for it. His eyes never left me as I followed Masters to a table near the far corner of the room. A fat man wearing a greasy apron moved from behind the bar and stood before our table.

'What'll it be, gents? Eating or drinking?'

'Eating and coffee,' Masters told him easily.

'That cash money or trading?'

The mention of cash had aroused the attention of the card players. Their game forgotten, they awaited the answer, and liked what they heard. As one they rose their feet and come towards us. The bartender backed off quickly.

'Not much cash money around these parts, mister. Been an age since I even seen any. Maybe you'd like to sit in on a game with us?'

'What you going to use for a stake?' Masters asked. 'I got no use for that many matches.'

'We got horses, saddles, guns,' the man told him, putting a lot of weight on the last word.

'Already got a horse, saddle, and a gun,' Masters said, adding his own weight to the last word. 'All we got need of right now is food and coffee. But just to keep things friendly, I reckon we could stake you to a bottle and maybe some grub.'

The bearded man smiled but I could still see the light of greed in his eyes. 'That's real friendly, mister. You heard the man, Beck. Three meals and a bottle.'

I watched them move back to their table. 'You're real generous with my money.'

The ghost of a smile touched his lips. 'Just buying us a little time, boy. Call it an investment, if you like. If I wanted to get real nasty, I'd have got you to cook the food for them.'

Masters smiled his thanks to a fat Indian squaw as she brought our food to us. She was the first Indian I'd ever seen, but her face was pleasant enough. I thanked her and her face broke into a real nice smile. I don't guess she got too many thanks for her efforts. Today was her lucky day. I'd even called her 'ma'am'. One of the three men snickered.

Her food was real good, too, best I'd had in a long time. There wasn't much dish-cleaning to do after Cole and me had finished eating. A white-faced pup brought a smile to my face as he wandered in from the back someplace moving towards the three men. A boot sent the pup whimpering towards me. I lifted him gently, feeling my blood run chill in my veins.

'Don't do that again, mister,' I warned. 'The pup wasn't doing no harm, just wanted a little attention.'

'Buying a man a little food and a bottle don't give you the right to threaten him, boy,' the bearded man said.

'Just saying it like it is, mister. He wasn't about

33

to tear your throat or nothing. I don't like to see nothing hurt that can't fight back.'

'You growed up enough to fight back, boy?'

I considered that for a while. I had had more than my share of fights along the way, never having learned to back up. Most of those fights had been caused because the other kids had heard talk of Jefferson Wilde and needed to find out if I was as tough as my old man. That was something else I owed him for. Fighting the land had given me a good width to my shoulders, a strong back, and power in my arms, but I was facing up to a full-growed man now. I had doubts.

'You follow your old man in one respect, boy,' Cole said: 'you sure know how to find trouble.'

It didn't look like I was going to get much help from Masters. He stayed seated as the bearded man got to his feet and came towards us. I put the pup safely aside and rose to my feet.

'He's carrying a lot of fat,' Cole said quietly. 'Take away his wind and you are half-way to beating him. Course I could be wrong, Watch your back. If you hurt him any, his friends will probably join in.'

'At least he's got friends,' I snapped.

'I asked you a question, boy,' the bearded man said, standing before me.

'Yeah, I'm growed up enough,' I told him, and hit him in the belly.

He hadn't expected that. The wind left him in a rush and I hit him again. If there were any rules in this fight I wasn't about to obey them. Stomping hard on his foot to bring his chin down shamed me some but I would live with it. My upper cut almost took his head off. His eyes glazed, and I stood back measuring the punch that dumped him on top of his friends' table. Don't know what got them angriest; me beating their friend or him spilling their rotgut when he landed on the table.

Satisfied that the bearded man's interest in the fight had waned some I moved back to face Cole Masters. He nodded his approval. 'You got more brains than I gave you credit for, kid. I like a dirty fighter.'

'He's bigger than me. Only did what I had to before he did it to me.'

'But you forgot something, boy. And that was the most important lesson.'

I started to ask him what it was when a heavy fist slammed alongside my head, driving me off my feet. I caught sight of two blurred figures standing over me and taste of a boot driving into my ribs before Masters got to his feet and looked down at me.

'Watch your back. Remember? I warned you.'

His elbow drove into the side of the face of the man nearest me as he stood on one leg aiming another kick at me. That brought a smile to my face. It was a lesson these men should have learned a long time ago. I got to my feet again as his long looping punch connected with the other man's face. It was a good punch, one I would have been proud of.

The man he had hit first was coming at me again but I held my hands up. 'I've had my fight. This one is his.'

Showing good sense, he didn't argue the point. The odds were better this way. Besides after they took Masters out of the picture they could settle with me. Pity I hadn't thought of that first. I could find myself in real trouble if the fight went against Masters.

I signalled to Beck for another cup of java as I watched the fight with relief growing inside of me. Cole Masters seemed to have the measure of the two men, even enjoying himself as those hard fists of his drove home with unerring accuracy. The two men were starting to lose interest in the fight and I couldn't blame them much. I could almost feel their pain as those fists of Masters connected. Unlike mine, there was a certain finesse in Cole Masters' fighting and it was paying off. Me, I knew only one way to fight, head down and go in swinging. It had worked with the bearded man, but I would be easy prey for someone like Cole Masters.

The first man went down – although I could swear the punch barely brushed him – and he decided to stay there. That took the fight out of the other man, too. He turned and walked away, stepping over the body of the man I had laid out. He was conscious now, but had no interest in what was happening around him. It would be a little while until he got all his senses back.

We left a few minutes later, me carrying the pup. It wasn't in me to leave that poor creature behind for those men to take their woes out on. Besides, I had me a liking for him. Generous to a fault with my money, Masters brought the three men another bottle before we left.

'I don't reckon we'll have money enough left to buy a wagon and supplies if you keep on buying booze for every deadbeat we meet along the way,' I complained as we rode away.

'Like I told you earlier, kid, we're buying time. Sure wish I could have bought us enough time for me to teach you how to use those guns of yours though. One bottle of rotgut isn't going to be much help to us. It won't do a lot to ease the anger inside them.'

I wasn't about to carry all the blame for what had taken place. 'I ain't about to stand by and let someone abuse a poor helpless animal.'

'The pup's got nothing to do with it, boy. It was plain to see what they had in mind the second you walked through that door back there in those new clothes of yours. To them it meant you had money in your pocket. If you had eyes to see and an ounce of sense in that head of yours you'd have seen one of those men slip outside to check on our horses. That new saddle and Winchester of yours only confirmed what they had in mind. They would have killed us just for those two items alone.'

There was sense in what he said and I cussed myself for not noticing it myself. The thought frightened me. I knew now what Cole Masters had in mind when he bought the whiskey for those men. If they had got drunk enough there was a chance they would have forgotten about us. But that chance was gone now. It wouldn't be just greed that would be driving those men now. They had a score to settle.

There would be shooting the next time we met, and I didn't even know how to use a gun. Hell, I already had five men on my tail, and I'd managed to pick up another three. That was plain greedy.

'I'm the one they're after. Maybe it's best if we split up,' I said. 'It's not your fight. They'll know which of us to follow.'

'Happen you're right, boy,' Masters argued, shaking me. 'Think you can stake me to a little grub and cash? If you chance to make it, you'll find me at a little town called Leeway on the Missouri.'

I stared at him in disbelief. I had made a noble gesture. It was up to him to respond in kind. This wasn't the way western men were supposed to act. Once a friendship was formed, that was it. There was no backing out. A man always stood by his friends. That was one of the unwritten codes of the frontier.

Reluctantly, I handed over some grub and thirty dollars in cash. Sure I was mad at him but I couldn't let any man go short, even one who would desert a friend at time of need.

I watched him ride away, wishing I had kept my big mouth shut. I had put the idea in his head. He was out of sight before I began cussing him good and loud. Maybe later, when I got to thinking about it, I would have forgiven him for riding away, but I doubted it. Without his help, I wouldn't have got this far. He had done me a favour, and I owed him for it, but he had also made me aware of my shortcomings. Knowing that I couldn't make it alone only served to tighten that cold fist of fear in my stomach.

The shadows were starting to lengthen now, each one a threat. The men coming up behind me would soon find my trail. Finding where Cole and I had parted company would bring a smile to their faces. All they would have to contend with was one greenhorn kid. Life couldn't be easier.

Four

The few tricks I had learned from Cole Masters came to my aid as I rode on. Even with the pup for company, I had never felt so lonesome in my life. Cole Masters had deserted me when I most had need of him, and I hadn't yet learned enough from him to shake those men off my trail. I was only delaying the inevitable, and I knew it. It could only have been a matter of time until those men caught up with me.

Already, it seemed, I could feel their breath on the back of my neck. Losing them was the only chance I had, and it was a mighty slim one. There would be no hope for me at all if it came to a shoot-out. Even if I could point my rifle in the right direction I wasn't sure if I would be able to stop my hand shaking long enough to pull the trigger.

There was something I knew that Cole Masters hadn't taught me: fear drains a man of all strength. There was nothing left inside me when I

41

finally reined to a halt atop a rise. It was as good a place as any, with a dozen or so trees to offer me some kind of protection if those men caught up with me before morning. From here I had me a commanding view of the country and had a chance to slip away down the other side of the rise if I caught sight of those pursuing me. There was no one in view. I told myself that maybe I had got lucky and lost them, but I didn't believe it.

The pup took to exploring the area while I unsaddled the sorrel. I felt the need for hot coffee to fill the void in my stomach, but I couldn't risk a fire. Already the sun had dipped behind the horizon. It would soon be full dark and a fire could be seen from miles away, leading the men right to me. Every second was precious now, and I wasn't about to do anything to hasten my demise. For the first time in my life I had money in my jeans, but I couldn't buy a single breath with it.

Having money had helped in setting those men on my trail but men like those would have killed me anyway just for my horse and saddle. I could feel the tremor in my hand as I chewed jerky, sharing it with the pup. A foolish kid had left his home to hunt down and kill a man. Now he was the hunted, scared and alone, with his own death closing in on him. Dark clouds scurried across the night sky as if trying to hide my shame from the moon and stars.

The chill night air persuaded the pup to try its luck at sharing my blankets with me. My sense of security had vanished along with Cole Masters. Cussing him made me feel a little better as the pup wormed its way in alongside me, perhaps feeling its own insecurity.

The sky fulfilled its promise of rain as the grey dawn broke, but it wasn't that that awakened me. The pup moved restlessly at my side, making feeble attempts at growling. I touched him, trying to calm him, and felt his hackles rising. He was hearing things that I couldn't. Maybe nothing more than a jack rabbit, but I couldn't take the chance.

Moving cautiously, carrying my rifle with me, I came up behind the nearest tree. My eyes searched the distance. As yet, there was nothing to see. The land was full of dips and hollows. If there had been men out there they could have been within a half a mile of me and still not been visible. I waited, feeling the tension grow inside me. At my side, the pup remained alert and growling as he looked into the distance. He was starting to lose patience with me. Trouble was coming and I was too blind, deaf or stupid to know it.

There was still no movement. If there were men out there, they were biding their time waiting for me to make the first move. Who they were, I didn't know. Kelp's men or the men from the trading post? The latter was more likely. Apart from men who wanted to kill me, it seemed like I was alone in the world. For a little while it looked like I had found me a friend, but as soon as things got a little rough he had gone his own carefree way, leaving me to handle things on my own.

The breath caught in my throat as two riders emerged from a dip in the land, closer than I would have liked. Two men only, but that didn't mean much. The other man could already be some place out of my sight. The two riders were splitting up as if they already had me spotted, and I had the feeling that the third man was making his move behind me. His bullet would have taken me out of the saddle if I had tried to break away. They had me trapped and there was no way out.

The Winchester in my hands was of small comfort. I knew which end the bullet came out of but that was about it. I hadn't even loaded the rifle or pistol. Mr Crawley had done the loading for me before I left home. Apart from my old single-shot rifle, I'd never fired a gun in my life. That cold hard rock of fear seemed to be growing in my gut as I struggled to lever a bullet into the chamber. I knew that the chances of me hitting anything were remote.

One of the riders tumbled from the saddle as I tried to line my rifle up on him. A split-second later, my numbed brain felt the echo of a shot. The second rider died a minute later, and I watched a lone rider emerge from a dip in the ground, holding a smoking rifle. My relief left me weak as I recognized Cole Masters. I was about to rise to my feet and shout a welcome to him when I remembered the third man. It wasn't likely that only two of those men had left the trading post to hunt us down. Men like those would always need the odds in their favour. That third man could have been closing in behind me at that very moment.

Being right did me no good at all. A bullet took a chunk of flesh from my left shoulder. I yelped and rolled desperately away as another bullet came too close for comfort. With no hope of hitting him, I sprayed as many bullets as I could in his direction. I was rewarded with a muffled curse and the sound of fast approaching hooves as Cole Masters came towards us at a run. There was time only for the briefest glimpse of the third man as he left in a hurry at sight of Cole coming into view. The odds were against him now, and he didn't like it.

We could hear his horse retreating into the distance as Cole reined to a halt. His eyes narrowed as he noticed the blood seeping through my shirt. 'Get a fire going, boy. I'll take care of that wound of yours as soon as I get back.'

He was gone before I had a chance to protest. Enough men had died today. The third man was no longer a threat to us. All he wanted was to get as far away from us as possible. It was starting to look as if Cole Masters had developed a taste for killing.

I listened for the sound of the shot that would tell me that Masters had added to his tally of dead men as I built the fire. This was a savage land but there was no need for the killing of a fleeing man. The coffee was boiling by the time Cole returned, but I hadn't heard another shot. He was silent as he unsaddled his own horse and the two others he had brought back with him. For a moment he considered hobbling the other two, but decided against it. The animals had been ridden hard and had no urge to go anywhere for a while.

'Your investment, boy,' he said, indicating the two new horses as he squatted by the fire. 'Pretty good returns on a couple of bottles of whiskey, huh?'

'How did you know they'd follow us?' I asked quietly. I was in debt to him again, and didn't like it. Every move he made only served to remind me just how green I was. Without Cole Masters' help and know-how I wouldn't even have survived that first day.

He shrugged. 'Some people read books. I read

46

men. After a while it becomes instinct. Sometimes it's the difference between life and death. When a man becomes over-confident he makes mistakes. When you told me it was your fight it gave me the excuse I needed. When they saw that we had split up it made things a lot easier for them; all they had to contend with was a green kid. All I had to do was ride along in their wake until they caught up with you. They never once considered checking their trail, and they paid the price for it.'

'And what if they hadn't found me?'

'Never occurred to me,' he said with more than a hint of sarcasm in his tone. 'That coffee ready yet?'

I filled his cup and handed it to him. Later he cleaned up my wound and announced that I would live. It was starting to burn like hell. Some men took a certain pride in being shot but I wasn't about to join their ranks. Being shot hurt. I told Masters I had put lead into the third man, wanting him to know that I wasn't as useless as he thought.

He shrugged. 'Accidents happen, kid. Knew a man who shot himself in the foot once but that wasn't what he was aiming at.'

'Wasn't no accident,' I told him. 'I was shooting at him.'

'Where was he hiding? Where did you hit him?'

'Over there,' I said, indicating a clump of

bushes, not telling him that I had shot in that direction because the pup was growling that way. 'Don't know where I hit him, but I heard him cuss.'

'The way I heard it, kid, you was throwing enough lead to wipe out half the population. Some of it had to head in the right direction. 'Course, it could have been a deflection that caught him.'

I hadn't considered that possibility but had to admit it could have happened that way.

'We'll rest up here until tomorrow,' he said. 'The horses need a rest and it will give me a chance to teach you a little something about guns. You can't keep on relying on accidents. The most important things to remember is never to take a gun lightly. It's the devil's own creation.'

'They came in handy today,' I reminded him.

'Only because there was no other way. When there is, I want you to look for it. A gun should always be the last resort. A man taught me that a long time ago. He taught me a lot of things. Most of what I know, in fact. I want to pass that knowledge on to you. Use it well.'

That was strange talk for a man with the same mission in life as myself – to kill Jefferson Wilde. One day, I thought, I would ask him his reason for wanting Jeff Wilde dead, but I doubted that I would get an answer.

It wouldn't have taken much for a man like

48

Kelp to hate another but Cole Masters was a different proposition. Killing would never come easy to him. He could, if he had wanted, have hunted down and killed the third man, adding another horse to our collection, but I was sure he hadn't. I wondered if Jefferson Wilde would have done the same.

My shooting lessons began with the Winchester after we had eaten, and went better than I had hoped. By noon I was hitting my target nine times out of ten. Cole seemed pleased by my progress, but I had the feeling that he didn't like what he was doing.

'You've got a keen eye, Jim, and a quick brain ... for shooting anyway,' he added before my head got to swelling. 'But that's with a rifle. A six-shooter is a different thing altogether. Using a Colt is as much a matter of instinct as anything, and I can't teach you that. In most situations where you have to use a Colt there isn't time to aim. All you can hope to do is clear leather faster than the man you are up against and point. It has to become second nature to you. There's never any time to think.'

'I've been practising my draw as I've been riding,' I told him. 'Getting pretty quick.'

He shook his head sadly. 'Wrong way round, kid. First you practise shooting. When you can hit what you are aiming at every time, then you start practising your draw, but always with an empty gun. That's what happened to that feller that shot himself in the foot.'

'What's it like to kill a man, Cole?' I asked quietly.

He was silent for a moment. 'Some men get a kick out of it. I'll promise you one thing, kid, if you ever get to feeling that way, I'll kill you myself.'

Five

Cole Masters' words still echoed in my mind as I caught my first ever sight of the Missouri. There was no hiding from the truth in what he said. If I ever found satisfaction in taking another man's life he would kill me. It was something to keep in mind as I stared at the Missouri. It was unlike anything I had ever seen before; wild and awesome as it fought its way to the mighty Mississippi. I could only watch and wonder at its power.

Leeway, the town itself, was a disappointment and I wondered what reason Cole could have had for going there. We passed through the town before we'd even realized we were there. It was little more than a dozen clapboard buildings, hardly a setting-off station for the wagon trains to Oregon. We found ourselves at a run-down shack about half a mile outside town. The stench of cheap whiskey greeted us as soon as we stepped inside the door. There was a bundle of rags on the bunk; as Cole gave it a shake, it awoke to be a man.

Bleary eyes looked at us for quite a while before coming into focus. 'Where the hell you been, Cole? Been a coon's age since I saw you last. Bring a bottle?'

'Had some business to attend to. No bottle. We've got us a trip to make. We need a wagon, a good man to handle it; someone who knows the Oregon trail.'

'Still trying, huh, Cole? Ain't it time you realized there's nothing you can do for me? It's too late. Sure, I know the trail. A man doesn't forget things like that. As for handling a wagon, forget it. The only thing I've handled for years is a bottle, and that's just the way I like it.'

His eyes focused on me. 'Who's the kid? Seems like I've seen that face before, a long time ago.'

'Maybe you have,' Cole told him quietly. 'I picked him up along the way. He was in need of help. He's looking for his no-good father, aims to pay him back for all the wrong he's done. I thought he deserved a chance to meet up with him. Seems like his pa had a dream a long time ago of settling in a place called Wild Horse Valley in Oregon. The kid reckons he'll find his old man there. You want to help us find the kid's pa, Cleave?'

The man struggled to his feet, and for the first time I noticed he was missing his left arm. What the hell was Cole Masters playing at? Even with two good arms this man would be of no use to us. He was nothing more than a drink-sodden reject.

'I asked you a question, Cleave: you want to help us find the kid's pa? 'Course, the first time I catch you with a bottle I'll throw you off the wagon and leave you behind.'

If the man heard the question he was ignoring it as he weaved towards me, stopping to look deep into my face. I had no liking for that. Even the smell of his breath was enough to get me drunk.

'What's your name, boy?'

'It ain't boy,' I told him. 'It's Jim Wilde.'

'The man you are looking for, what's his name?'

'Jefferson Wilde. He's my father, but I ain't proud of that fact.'

'You got no reason to be, boy,' he snapped, turning to face Cole Masters. 'Damn you, Cole. I told you that was a name I never wanted to hear again. What did you bring him here for?'

'I don't know of anyone else who's even seen or heard of Wild Horse Valley. The kid's got a right to meet up with his pa. You want to deny him that chance, Cleave? Like it or not, I figure Jefferson Wilde owes him, and it's time he paid his dues.'

Without looking at me, the man said, 'The way I hear it, boy, Jefferson Wilde has been out of your life for a long time. It's better left that way. Why go looking for him now?'

'Because I aim to kill him,' I told him flat out.

'That figures. If ever a man deserved killing it's Jefferson Wilde. Cole been teaching you to use that gun on your hip?'

I nodded, and the slightest hint of a smile touched his lips. 'Well, that puts you in with a chance. Only ever knowed one man better with a gun than Cole Masters, and that's the man you're hunting.'

His eyes looked around at the shack, as if seeing it for the first time, and not liking what he was seeing. 'Should be pretty interesting when you finally meet up with Jefferson Wilde. Things have been getting pretty dull around here for a long time now, or maybe I just ain't been noticing. Got the idea they've even taken to watering my drink. You have anything to do with that, Cole?'

Masters grinned his acknowledgement of the fact.

Cleave shook his head. 'Thought it wasn't having the effect it once had. Keep getting memories and a growing dislike for myself. That ain't the way booze is supposed to work. Getting so I could hardly live with myself. Where's the money coming from to make this trek? Need a good wagon and plenty of supplies.'

'The kid sold his farm,' Cole told him. 'Might

even advance you enough for some decent clothing and a bar of soap if you asked him nice. But that depends on whether you decide to come along with us or not.'

'Don't see how you can find Jefferson Wilde without me,' Cleave said cryptically, and I got the feeling that he and Cole had a secret that they wasn't about to share with me.

'Holby's got a wagon for sale,' Cleave said. 'Wants a hundred dollars for it, but I reckon I can talk him down. Trust me with that much money, boy?'

I looked at Cole, and he nodded. 'Drunk or sober, his word is good, Jim.'

Reluctantly, I handed over the money before Cleave pushed us outside, saying he wanted to get cleaned up a little before doing business with Holby.

'Any more deadbeats you want to pick up along the way?' I snapped at Cole as soon as we were clear of the shack. 'What damned use is a one-armed whiskey soak to us? He's more likely to buy himself a share in a whiskey still than he is to get us a wagon. Right now, he's probably climbing out of a back window and making his way to the nearest saloon.'

'You haven't got much faith in your fellow man, have you, Jim? He'll get us a wagon and he'll get us to where we are going. My words won't teach

you anything about Cleave Devlin. That's something you are going to have to learn for yourself,
if you are big enough. Besides, I figure he's earned
the right to meet up with Jefferson Wilde again.'

Things were starting to get out of my reach.
Most of the talk inside the shack seemed to have
some kind of double-meaning that I couldn't
understand. They knew things that I didn't and
they weren't about to share that information with
me. They had their own reasons for meeting up
with Jeff Wilde and made it plain that it was none
of my damned business. All I knew for sure was
that I had teamed up with another man who had
reason to hate him. I was starting to wonder if I
was ever going to meet up with someone who
actually liked him.

I shrugged it aside. Cole Masters had promised
me the first chance at Jefferson Wilde, and that
was all I cared about.

The pup had finished its exploration of the yard
and come back to me when the door of the shack
opened and Cleave stepped out. His clothes had
seen better days but seemed clean. It would take
more than clothes to make Cleave Devlin into a
man again, if such a thing was possible. I still had
my doubts about him.

'Thought about taking a shave, but didn't figure
I was up to that yet,' he said sheepishly. 'Maybe
when my hand steadies up a little.'

'We passed a barber shop in town,' I said. 'You can use some of that money you intend saving on the wagon for a shave, some decent clothes and whatever else you're in need of.'

'You can take it out of my pay, boy. You do intend paying me, don't you?'

That thought hadn't occurred to me. 'I'm paying for the wagon, supplies and everything else we need. I reckon that's enough. You've got your reasons for going to Oregon. I got mine. If you want to try and make it on your own that's OK by me.'

'Don't reckon I got much choice then, do I? Where did the other two horses come from?'

Cole grinned. 'The kid's got a knack for getting himself into trouble. Ever since I met up with him he's had someone on his trail, but he wasn't satisfied with that. He had to pick up three more. We got rid of the last three, but the others aren't going to be so easy.'

'Anyone I know?' Cleave asked thoughtfully.

'Kelp and his bunch.'

'That's bad news. They're tough to handle, and Kelp's like a hound dog on the trail. What are they after, kid?'

'The same as us – Jefferson Wilde. They reckon I know where to find him. I didn't like the idea of them watching the farm every day so I sold up and lit out. Besides, I figure I've earned first chance at Wilde.'

'A lot of men would dispute that claim, boy,' Cleave said, moving to get a closer look at our spare horses. 'The roan ain't bad. Couple of days easy travelling would put the fire back in him. I could use him. The saddle, too. Any objections?'

There were no objections. I liked that roan, didn't want to part with it anyhow. Already I could sense a change in the man, as if he had made up his mind about something and intended seeing it through to the bitter end. Maybe I was wrong about him. Seemed like his hatred for Jefferson Wilde was even stronger than his taste for whiskey.

A little stiffly, he climbed into the roan's saddle and we headed back towards town. Already it looked like he was in charge, and Cole and me were just along for the ride. The first stop was at the store where he came out carrying an armful of clothes with a new Stetson balanced on top. It was my money he was spending but I said nothing. If we were to have joined up with a wagon train along the way, at least I wouldn't have been shamed by his appearance. He disappeared into the barber shop next door, still carrying the clothes.

There was a new look to Cleave Devlin when he emerged again, clean shaven, with his hair cut, and wearing his new duds. He seemed taller now and clear eyed, as if he knew where he was going.

He spread his new coat wide as he faced us. 'Only one thing missing now, Cole. Reckon that loan you're making me will extend to buying some weapons, kid? There's a pretty good rifle on the roan's saddle. I can use that, but I'll have need of a short gun.'

Cole unwrapped his bedroll and took out a Colt .45 and holster. 'Think this will suit you?'

'That's my gun. Where did you get it?'

'You gave it to me five years ago in exchange for a few bottles of whiskey. Remember? I've been taking care of it ever since.'

'Never gave up hope on me, did you, Cole? You could have been wrong; you still could be.'

'That's something we are going to have to find out for ourselves. You know what lies ahead of us. Think you can handle it?'

'Nope. If I had any sense I'd climb right back inside a whiskey bottle now.'

Again I had the feeling that they were talking around me, saying things they didn't want me to understand. Yet, in some obscure way, I was part of it. How, I didn't know.

The only thing I could understand was his look of disgust as he fastened his gun around his waist. It was now a part of him yet, for some strange reason, he wanted no part of it.

Six

The land stretched before us, seemingly endless and barren of life. Only the long grass moved, as if in time to the music of the wind that only it could hear. Almost a week had passed since we had left Leeway. There had been neither sight nor sign of another human being. It was an uncomfortable feeling, as if we were the only people left in the world.

Cleave Devlin handled the wagon and his team of hand-picked horses with an ease that I could never have hoped to match, but I was having doubts about him as a trail-finder. We had need to join up with a wagon train to stand any real chance of making it all the way to Oregon.

We had heard talk of a wagon train leaving Independence before we left Leeway, but we should have caught up to them before now. It was starting to look as if Cole Masters had put too much faith in his old friend's ability. Maybe he hadn't taken into consideration the years of whiskey. I had heard that hard drink destroyed a lot of brain cells. Don't know what my excuse would be, I thought wryly.

I rode up on the wagon seat with Devlin now, having no wish for the man's company, but heeding Cole's suggestion that I should learn how to handle the wagon in case I had need to. The main thing was getting to know your team, and Devlin had chosen them well, I admitted grudgingly. My sorrel was hitched alongside Devlin's roan on the tailgate. The sorrel finally had a name: Dancer. Flip, the pup, sat on my lap, not liking the tall grass waving at us as we passed.

'Can't understand it, boy,' Cleave said suddenly. He had hardly spoke a word to me since I climbed into the wagon seat. 'We should have caught up to that train by now. Either they've run into some kind of trouble or their guide isn't up to the job.'

'Maybe we've got the same problem,' I suggested.

He looked at me sharply. 'Still got a lot to prove to you, haven't I, boy? Think I've still got a bottle hidden away some place?'

'If you have, I can't find it,' I said. 'And I ain't a boy.'

'You are to me, until you prove different.

Physically, you're growing but, inside, all you've got is a lot of hate and self-pity. They stunt a man's growth.'

'What makes you any better? You hate Jefferson Wilde just as much as I do. That's the reason you're here.'

'I got reason to hate him; more reasons than you could shake a stick at, and it goes back a lot further than yours does. Just one difference between us, boy: I don't *want* to face up to Jefferson Wilde. It's just something I have to do.'

He was silent then, his eyes searching the distance, without missing anything. I focused my gaze on Cole Masters riding on ahead and kept the bit between my teeth. Cleave Devlin was too near the edge for my liking. One more wrong word from me could push him over.

Making up his mind suddenly, he reined the team to a halt. 'I'm going to scout ahead. Make camp here for a while until I return. I'll send Cole back with you.'

'I don't need a nursemaid. Take Cole with you.'

'I don't need him, you might. This is Indian country. Kiowa, Comanche. Alone, you'd be easy pickings for them. No sense in tempting fate. 'Course, you could use the smell of your cooking to drive them off.'

He was aboard his roan and riding away before I had chance to think up a smart answer. But I

63

was sure grateful to climb down from that hard wagon seat.

Over two hours had passed before Cleave Devlin returned, his face tight as he dismounted, leaving the roan ground-hitched as he made his way to the coffee pot.

'Found that train we're looking for,' he said shortly. 'Pretty big, judging by the tracks. That's the only reason they've stayed alive so long. They've got a bunch of hostiles on their tail.'

'How many?' Cole asked.

'Not enough to make an attack but they sent out a man in search of reinforcements. It don't seem like the train is expecting trouble. At most, I reckon they've got twenty-four hours before the Indians attack. There's a chance we can reach that train and lend a hand before the attack, if we push hard. Our other choice is to stay out of it.'

I was on my way to hitch up the team before he had finished speaking. The way I saw it we had no choice. There were women and kids aboard that train. If we didn't try to help them their blood would be on our hands, too.

'You two ride on ahead and warn them. I'll come behind with the wagon. It's the best way. The two of you would be of more use in a fight than me.'

There seemed to be some kind of mist in Cleave's eyes as he looked at me, and I wondered if he had taken a bottle with him when he went in search of the wagon train.

'Seems like the decision has been made for us, Cole,' he said, his voice throaty. 'It's the right decision, Jim, but you haven't thought it all out yet. You'd be alone then, and those redskins could come along at any time.'

'That's a chance I'll have to take. Those folks in the wagon train won't have no chance at all if you don't get to them first.'

He shook his head. 'We ride in together. Right now, those Indians have got surprise on their side. We have to turn that around. My plan was to tag along behind the train, fool those hostiles into thinking we're stragglers trying to catch up. We make it look like we don't know there's an Indian within a hundred miles of us. If it works they'll let us through because they won't want to alert the wagon train.

'They'll have nothing to gain by attacking us. With luck, they'll wait until their reinforcements arrive and try to take us all out in one raid. Leastways, that's the way it's supposed to work. They may have other ideas.'

If there was a flaw in his plan I didn't want to go looking for it. It was going to be scary riding along in the wake of the wagon train knowing hostile eyes would be watching us. Pretending we didn't know was going to be the hardest part, but that was something else I didn't want to think about.

Finding the wagon tracks was easy now that we knew where to look, but we had to start a long way back to make it look right. Within a half-hour I could feel those dark cruel eyes on us as I rode in the wagon seat with Cleave. It was the best place to be. Like the man or not, he had a reassuring presence that helped quell some of the panic rising in me. My rifle was in easy reach, just behind the seat.

'Feel them, Jim?' he asked.

'Feel something,' I said. 'Picked it up a few minutes ago, a kind of chill. Thought maybe it was my imagination or just plain fear.'

'Good. It means that you've got something going for you that makes you right for this kind of country. Felt the same way myself on my first trek into Indian country. Kind of sick inside and doubting that I would have guts enough to face up to whatever was coming my way.'

I wanted to tell him that I wasn't scared and I was ready to face a thousand Indians if it came down to it, but we would both have known it was a lie.

'Isn't a man born that hasn't known fear of some kind, Jim. And each one of us has run away from something at one time or another. Some of us are still running.'

I got the feeling that he was trying to tell me something but seemed reluctant to find the right words. Both he and Cole were hiding things from me, as if thinking I wasn't yet growed up enough to handle the truth. But knowing that he, too, had known fear helped ease some of the shame in me. But the doubts remained. If he was wrong about the Indians attacking us we wouldn't live long enough even to catch sight of the wagon train.

I was having some doubts about myself, too, wondering if I would be any use in a fight. Cole Masters was the only reason I was still alive. Knowing he was riding close by helped.

Cleave glanced at me strangely, as if trying to read my thoughts. 'None of us ever really knows what we will do when it comes right down to it, Jim,' he said softly. 'Life is that way. Most of us ride the wind, never knowing where it is taking us. Seeds on the wind, that's all we are. Some of those seeds land on good ground and grow strong. Others wither or remain stunted for the rest of our lives.'

I wished I knew what he was talking about but now wasn't the time to think about it. 'You think I'm scared, don't you?'

A half-smile touched his face. 'Why should you be the exception? I already had one haircut this year. I figure it's short enough already.'

I found myself answering his grin. In spite of

myself I was starting to like Cleave Devlin. He was never going to be the man Cole Masters made him out to be, but he was fighting an uphill battle against booze and the loss of his arm; he was trying hard and I had to admire him for it.

'Maybe you'd feel a little easier if you carried that Winchester of yours. Cole reckons you're pretty good with it. And it could help discourage those Indians out there from trying anything with their bows. Knowing that you have a rifle to hand should remind them that the hint of an attack will bring some lead coming their way and blow their hopes of a sneak attack on the wagon train.'

He shook his head sadly before adding wryly, 'Should have thought of that earlier. I guess easy living and hard booze takes the edge off a man.'

Casual like, I reached behind the wagon seat and brought the Winchester into view. He was right; having the rifle to hand did make me feel a lot easier. Making it look like I wasn't aware of the hostile eyes watching us was the hardest part.

'How far ahead of us do you reckon the train is?' I asked, not liking the lengthening shadows closing about us. I had heard that Indians didn't like fighting at night – something about their souls being forced to wander in eternal darkness if they got killed at night – but I set no store by it. Could be there were Indians who didn't believe it either, and it would be just my luck to come across an atheist Indian.

'About an hour, I'd say,' Cleave answered. 'They've set up camp. I can smell woodsmoke in the air.'

The pup, too, was aware that we weren't alone in the closing night as we pushed on. Every foot of this journey was starting to seem like a mile. Try as I might, I still couldn't detect the scent of woodsmoke on the air. Could be it was just wishful thinking on Cleave's part or he was just trying to make me feel easier. He had been around a long time, much of that time spent fighting Indians and travelling. Out-guessing hostiles had become second nature to him. But the years of hard-drinking could have taken its toll.

Even now, the Ute's reinforcements could have been moving between us and the wagon train. If that had been the case, I would have died with just one regret: that I hadn't been able to take Jeff Wilde with me.

Seven

The night was silent, quieter and somehow darker than any I had ever known before. Each shadow was a threat. It seemed like the world was already mourning our deaths. No one, I thought, would ever know that Jim Wilde had died out here in the middle of nowhere; there would be no one to speak fine words over me, even if those words would have been lies. All I had to show for my life was a lot of hard work for nothing, and hate still burning inside me for a man who was little more than a fleeting shadow in my past.

As far back as I could remember, hate had been the only real emotion I had known. And killing Jefferson Wilde my only ambition. It was starting to look like that ambition was about to die with me tonight.

The silence was starting to get to me; it was making me look too deep inside myself, and I didn't like what I saw.

71

'I've heard that Indians don't like fighting at night,' I said quietly.

'That's Apaches, kid, but I've never known one that wouldn't take a life at any time of day if it was on offer. The first thing to learn about fighting Indians is to figure out what they'll do, but always to expect something different. There's only one thing an Indian respects, and that's a brave man.'

He lifted his head as if testing the air. 'We're close, almost within sight of the wagon train.'

For the first time I was smelling the woodsmoke. Seemed like the train was camped just over the next rise. But our troubles wouldn't be ending there. Somewhere in the night a whole posse of Utes was heading our way.

Surprised faces greeted us as we rode into the circle of wagons. One man with an open friendly face stepped forward as Cleave and I stepped down from the wagon. Cole had already dismounted and was unsaddling his horse.

'Kind of strange to find a lone wagon way out here,' the man said.

'We've been looking for you for most of a week,' Cleave said. 'You're a long way off the trail.'

'Brinkley's idea. He's the wagon boss. Thought we could avoid a lot of trouble that way.'

'He was wrong,' Cleave told him flatly. 'This is Ute country. Best if you get back on the trail as soon as possible, if you get the chance.'

'You trying to take over my job, mister?' a tall hefty man said, moving out from the bunch surrounding us.

'If I had your job, you wouldn't be in the mess you are in right now, mister,' Cleave said. 'You've put a lot of lives at risk, including women and kids.'

'If you mean Indians, mister, there isn't a redskin within fifty miles of this place. I'd smell them if there were.'

'There are about a dozen Utes watching you right now,' Cleave answered. 'And more on the way. It's my guess that they'll be here by morning.'

'This is my wagon train, mister,' Brinkley snapped, 'and you ain't welcome here. I suggest you move on right now.'

His right hand hovered over his gunbutt, making it plain that he wasn't giving Cleave any choice in the matter. Two other men, cut from the same cloth as Brinkley, came across to side him.

A slight smile touched Cleave's face, and I got the impression that he had been in this kind of situation before, but this was probably the first time he ever welcomed it. This time he felt that he had something to prove, if only to himself. And that empty sleeve tucked into his belt had a lot to do with it.

I didn't even see his hand move as it lashed out

catching Brinkley full in the face and landing him on his rear end.

The other two men were starting to make their moves when Cole Masters' quiet voice stopped them.

'That would be a mistake, boys.'

One glance at the tall, loose-limbed man convinced Brinkley's friends that they should tend to their own business. Cole Masters was a different proposition to a one-armed man. Their ignoring me, ruffled my pride a little. I was nobody, just a still wet-behind-the-ears kid, and no threat to them.

Cleave stood over Brinkley, his face and voice tight. 'I should kill you, mister, for putting all these folks in danger but, come tomorrow, I'll need every gun I've got.'

The man who had first greeted us stepped forward. 'The name's Amos Blaine, mister. I kind of organized this train. I think we should hear what you've got to say.'

Cleave's chest heaved as the violence abated inside him. 'I already said it, Mr Blaine. You've had about a dozen Utes on your trail for the past couple of days. They're just waiting for a big war-party to arrive before they make their raid. The only reason they let us through was because we pretended we didn't know they were out there, and they didn't want to alert you. They figure it's best to take us all out together. That answer all your questions?'

'All but one,' Blaine answered. 'How come you bought into this thing? You could have slipped away easy while the Utes concentrated on us.'

'That's a pretty dumb question, Blaine. Take a look about you. What do you see? I see women and kids. If we had done what you just suggested we would have been seeing those women and kids for the rest of our miserable lives. No faces, only shadows and voices calling for our help.'

'You're right, mister. It was a stupid question. My first stupid mistake was hiring Brinkley, Sims and Gibson as scouts. It could have been my last mistake, if you hadn't come along.'

'It could still be your last mistake,' Cleave told him. 'I don't know how many Utes are heading this way, but it's a sure bet that we'll be outnumbered. We need some kind of plan to cut those odds down.'

'We can talk about it over coffee after we eat. My wife is a good cook, and you look like you need some grub inside you.'

'We'll get the talking done first, Mr Blaine,' Cleave said. 'Might not have the time later. Cole Masters here will choose the men he wants on guard duty tonight. I don't think they are ready to hit us, but I don't want to take any chances either. First thing is to let those fires die back some. I don't want the Utes to see any more than they have to.'

'If there *are* any 'skins out there,' Brinkley said, finally deciding it was safe for him to regain his feet. 'Could be you're trying to take over this train for some reason of your own.'

'Because of you, my life is on the line now too,' Cleave told him. 'I reckon that gives me reason to have some say in it. You object to that, Brinkley?'

There was a challenge in his words, but Brinkley wasn't about to accept yet. He didn't know enough about Cleave Devlin. 'I don't know you, mister, but I've been hearing Cole Masters' name for a while now. That's the kind of trouble I don't want. Still find it kind of strange that we haven't seen hair or hide of any Utes though.'

'That's the way they like it, Brinkley. You'll see them when the time is right. 'Course you can always go out looking for them, if you want.'

'I can wait,' Brinkley answered. 'I like to know what I'm up against first. Like I said, Cole Masters I've heard of. You got a name I might know?'

'Cleave Devlin, but that won't mean a thing to you – yet.'

'You're right, Devlin. It don't mean a damned thing to me. Doubt if it ever will.'

For the first time Brinkley let his gaze rest on me. He had learned a measure of respect from

Cleave's hard fist and the name of Cole Masters was known to him, so that just left me. It was plain to see that I was new to the country. Nothing but a green kid way out of his depth in a world of violence. But he had already made one mistake today. This time he had to be sure.

'Who's the maverick? Looks like you found him some place along the way. Maybe you should have left him there.'

I could feel the blood rush to my face. All eyes were on me now. No one expected Cleave or Cole to step in for me. This was a man's country, each one expected to fight his own fights. But this fight wouldn't be with fists. Brinkley had already proved that he couldn't take a punch.

He had failed in his attempt to buffalo Cleave and he wasn't about to take on Cole Masters. True to his type, he was picking on the weakest of the bunch to restore some of his lost respect. If it came down to a shooting I would lose. That much I knew.

'He's proved his worth so far,' Cleave said quietly. 'His name's Jim Wilde. Mean anything to you?'

'Wilde? Any kin to Jefferson Wilde?'

'His son,' Cleave told him. 'That make a difference, Brinkley?'

It was Brinkley's turn to flush. Jefferson Wilde's name had become part of folklore. Sure, his name hadn't been spoken for a long time but, for all he knew, Jefferson Wilde could have been right with me all that time, passing on his gun skills to me.

Jeff Wilde's name had spread further than I would have believed possible. It was the kind of notoriety I didn't want, but I was part of that fame, whether I liked it or not, and Cleave had just used it to avoid a gunfight. Brinkley couldn't hide the doubt on his face. Deciding the risk was too great, he turned on his heel and walked away. The wagon train now belonged to Cleave.

'We'll take you up on that offer of food, Blaine, as soon as we attend to our animals,' Cleave said.

I caught sight of a dark-haired girl near the Blaine wagon. For some reason, my glance lingered, holding her in my eyes a little too long. There had never been any girls in my life; there had never been room or time. The arrangement suited me. I offered to take care of the animals while Cleave and Cole went to supper, but – whether they knew my reasons or not – they were having none of it.

Reluctantly, I followed them to the Blaine wagon. The girl was there. Just sight of her took my breath away. Those direct blue eyes kept watching me as I hunched over my food, seeming to look direct into my soul. A half-smile played about her lips. All thoughts of the Utes were forgotten – I was in far more danger from this girl.

Cole, too, seemed aware of all the attention I was getting and he was enjoying my discomfort. I kept my attention on my food and the pup at my side. It was good food, the best I'd eaten for a long time, but I wasn't enjoying it. Mr Blaine had introduced his wife and daughters to us before we sat down to eat. Lindy was the elder of the two girls. About eighteen, I guessed, and past marrying age in this country. Most girls were married not too long after their sixteenth birthday.

Seemed like Lindy was the picky type, needing to find the right man before settling down. Well, she couldn't have been too fussy if she had set her sights on me. So far, she hadn't said anything to me but that half-smile or hers told me more than I wanted to know.

Milly, about four years younger than her sister, also seemed to take pleasure from my uneasiness and was determined to make the most of it. She sat near me, not saying anything, but letting me know what she was thinking. Finally breaking the silence, she asked the pup's name. I told her after two attempts. Right now, I wished I was back out there among the Utes. Looked like both girls were out to make my life as miserable as possible.

79

I needed to get back to my wagon. At least there was some measure of safety there. I got to my feet, thanking Mrs Blaine for the vittles, but Cleave stopped me leaving.

'There's still some talking to be done, Jim. Men talk, and you are part of it. We need some kind of plan to cut the odds in our favour.'

Blaine looked pointedly at his wife and daughters and they moved away to join a group of women at another wagon. He poured fresh coffee for each of us before speaking. 'What kind of odds are we talking about?'

Cleave shrugged. 'Not good. We can expect to be outnumbered two or three to one, and they'll have the choice of where to hit us. They could wipe us out without a shot being fired in return.'

'Then we have to make that choice for them,' I said, feeling I should add something to the conversation.

'I think they'll come to us without us issuing an invitation, kid,' Blaine said. 'I'd rather avoid that if we can.'

'They'll be coming at us whether we invite them or not,' I said, feeling foolish. I hadn't worked out a full plan yet. All I had was the germ of an idea. 'It was Cleave's plan really. I thought we could stretch it out a bit further by keeping on pretending we don't know they are out there. It worked once. No reason why it shouldn't work again. We make it look easy for them to attack us. When they do...'

Cole grinned as he looked at Cleave. 'Told you the kid had a good head on his shoulders. He don't use it that often, but ... it could work. I got nothing better in mind anyhow. We wait right here for them. There's a lot of open ground around us, giving us a clear field of fire. If we take out enough of them on the first wave it could discourage them from trying another attack.'

Cleave nodded agreement. 'Just a couple of problems that I can see. First, we won't know when the reinforcements arrive. We need that information.'

Cole's grin broadened. 'I guess that's down to us, unless you can't cut it any more. Things could get pretty rough out there. But I'll be there to hold your hand.'

'Best if you stay on the right side of me then. I ain't got but one hand, in case you hadn't noticed,' Cleave said with the hint of a smile. I had the feeling that this was the first time he had been able to laugh about his disability and it felt good. He was starting to accept his handicap and beginning to feel like a man again.

They started talking about needing a reason for staying here that the Utes would understand, and I came up with a suggestion for a prayer meeting. After a little thought they agreed with my plan.

81

'Maybe we can add to it a little,' Cleave said. 'Give the Utes something they can really understand. Time we had a look at what we are up against. You'll be running things until we get back, Jim.'

Me? I knew as much about Indians as I knew about dancing. 'You've got the wrong man for the job. Mister Brinkley won't like it. He's supposed to be wagon boss.'

'Not any more. He's made too many mistakes,' Cleave said. 'Just one could prove fatal. We don't get too many second chances out here. If you get any trouble off him let us know when we get back. We'll handle it.'

'Maybe we should make that clear to Brinkley before we set out,' Cole suggested. 'Could save Jim a bit of bother.'

I watched them talk to Brinkley and his friends; their stance made it plain that the three of them could expect real trouble if they went against orders.

Eight

For the first time since we had set out I was beginning to doubt Cleave's judgement. Maybe the years of hard drinking had unsettled his brain. He had appointed me guardian of the train. There were a lot of lives in my hands and they weighed heavy.

I tried to pierce the black night with my eyes and failed. Cleave and Cole could have been roasting over the Ute fire, but I doubted it. Neither man would have been taken without a fight. I had no idea how well Cleave could use a pistol but he carried it like it belonged there. And he was a lot smarter than I had first given him credit for. So far the only dumb thing he had done was to put me in charge of the wagon train.

The voice startled me – so much for my sixth sense – and I turned quickly to find Lindy standing behind me. 'I asked if there was any sign of them?' she repeated.

'Nope, and you shouldn't be here,' I answered sharply. I needed to keep my mind on other things. She was a distraction I couldn't afford right then.

My tone upset her. 'I just thought you needed someone to talk to. You're only a boy and Mr Devlin has given you a big job to do. You're afraid, and you lack the courage to admit it.'

I was angry with her, but didn't really know why. All I knew was she was getting under my skin and I didn't like it. For half my life I had plotted the course I needed to follow. I was set on that course now and couldn't allow anything to alter it.

'Right now you scare me more than the Utes do,' I told her bluntly. 'Don't know what you've got in your mind, but I can't let anything or anyone stop me doing it.'

Taken aback she could only stare at me for a couple of minutes. 'You really do think a lot of yourself, don't you? Well let me tell you that you are no prize, Jim Wilde.'

'Wouldn't sell a ticket if I was,' I agreed. 'I just thought you should know how it is with me. In time you'll realize that I've done you a favour. At the moment all I am to you is someone who came riding up at a time of trouble, but that doesn't make me no hero. I don't even know if I've got courage enough to face up to what's ahead of us.

84

You'll find a different kind of man to me up in Oregon. Doubt if there's one up there that wouldn't ride a week just to catch a glimpse of you.'

The anger died in her eyes. 'I'll accept that as a compliment, but you won't be one of those men, will you?'

'I'll have other things on my mind. When you find out just what those things are you'll come to know just how big a favour I've done you. I won't like myself any more than you will then, but I'll learn to live with it.'

'If it's so bad, why do it?'

'It's a promise I made myself a long time ago. I can't back away from it now.'

'Do you want to tell me about it?'

'No. You shouldn't even be here. It's time you went back to your wagon and stayed there.'

An impish smile touched her face. 'Thinking of my safety – or your own?' She started to leave then, pausing only to look over her shoulder with a parting shot. 'We may be more alike than you think, Jim Wilde. When I make my mind up about something, I don't give up on it, either.'

Only when she had passed from sight did the full intent of her words hit, but that made no sense. Why would someone who looked like her want to saddle herself with a no-hoper like me?

'Sounds like you've found yourself some

trouble,' Cleave said, coming from behind the wagon. I hadn't even known he was anywhere near.

'I didn't hear you coming in. Guess I should learn to keep my mind on the business in hand.'

'You weren't supposed to hear me,' he said. 'If you had I'd have been very disappointed in myself. Cole is still out there. Should be in soon. Any coffee to hand? Getting kind of chilly out there.'

He poured out some coffee, squatting on his heels before speaking again. 'They've got their reinforcements. Near enough forty warriors is the best I could tally. We're going to have need of your plan.'

I was beginning to have doubts about that plan now. What if it didn't work? I'd be responsible for the deaths of a lot of people. The Utes were out there but, unseen as they were, I hadn't really been able to accept them as a danger to us. Maybe I was just hoping that the reinforcements would never arrive. It wasn't to be, and the threat was now real, hanging over us like a thunder cloud.

'Miss Blaine seems to be a very determined young lady. Never known a man to slip a noose thrown by a pretty girl yet. Sure they fight it for a while but that noose keeps getting tighter until...'

There was no need for him to say any more. He

was talking like I was roped, hog-tied and branded already, but it wasn't to be that way. 'You don't know me, Cleave. Fact is, I don't even know myself yet. The only thing I am sure of is that I'm not the marrying kind. I don't want to be tied down to any woman for the rest of my life. I told her so.'

He grinned. 'Sure you did, but was she listening? Females got a habit of only listening to things they want to hear. It's a mistake to tell them that you're not interested. That's a challenge to their womanhood, and one they can't resist.'

I hadn't thought of it that way; never would have done until Cleave had pointed it out. As I recalled now there had been a determination in Lindy's eyes after I had said my piece. I cussed myself for a fool. I knew nothing about women; I'd never learned how to handle them. All I could hope for now was to avoid Lindy as much as possible in the future, if I still had a future after tomorrow.

'Which direction do you think they'll come from?' I asked without really wanting to know. There was a bag of worms inside me, each squirming to get free and each one representing a new doubt or fear. Most of those fears and doubts were about myself and how I would react to the situation when it came about.

'North,' he said quietly. 'There's a dip in the land they can use to keep out of sight until they get within striking distance of us. If your plan is going to work every man of us will need to be ready. They'll need to seize their chance; as far as they know, they'll never have a better opportunity to catch us off guard.'

He stopped talking to pour an extra cup of coffee. How he knew that Cole was coming in I couldn't even guess at, but suddenly he was there besides us taking the cup into his work-toughened hands.

'What's your tally?' he asked Cleave.

'About forty, give or take. Looks like Red Wolf will be leading the charge.'

Cole swore. 'That's who it was. Thought I recognized the chief but I couldn't get close enough to put a name to him. I had hoped he'd retired by now, let one of his sons take over. He's a wily old coot. Hasn't lost too many battles in his life. We can't afford any mistakes against him.'

'I want about a dozen men hidden in the wagons ready to meet the charge and give us time enough to get to our weapons. You choose the men you want. Make sure they know what they're doing. No itchy trigger-fingers. I want those Utes as close as possible before we open fire.'

Cole nodded agreement, and I pitied any man who dared to pull a trigger before he gave the order.

I was alone. Cleave had wandered off to explain the plan to Blaine and the others. Cole had gone along to pick the men he wanted. The burden of responsibility weighed heavy on my shoulders. I should have kept my big mouth shut, let Cleave and Cole work out their own plan. Let them carry the burden of guilt. It was their fault anyway. They shouldn't have listened to me. That made me feel a little better, but I knew there wouldn't be any sleep for me that night.

Dawn streaked the sky before I was even aware of it. I had cat-napped through part of the night without knowing it. I had never known that fear could drain a man of all his strength that way. Cleave and Cole were already making breakfast when I climbed from my blankets but I had no stomach for food this day. I doubted that I could even hold it down.

Only the tension in Cleave's shoulders showed that his mind was also on the Utes as he passed me a mug of coffee. I needed that, but refused his offer of breakfast. I felt Cole's strong hand on my shoulder. 'None of us really knows how we are going to face up to a challenge until we meet it, Jim. The only sure thing is that none of us can escape through life without facing one head on.'

'You think I'm scared, don't you?' I said angrily, wanting to put him straight. It was one thing to admit to myself that I was afraid, but another thing to admit it to the likes of Cole Masters and Cleave Devlin.

'If you're not, kid, then you are the only one on this train that isn't.'

Knowing that my fear was shared made me feel a little less lonesome, but I still had my doubts about my ability to cope with a horde of Utes coming at me.

'Besides you've got other things to think about,' Cole said. 'You've been elected to hold the prayer meeting. Everyone thought you'd be the best man for the job. I bragged you up a bit, said you talked up a real mean sermon. Don't prove me wrong, Jim. You are going to have to speak up good and loud so Cleave and me can hear you in the wagons.'

That took my breath away. Me making a sermon? Sure, I had attended church with Ma, but my mind had always been on other things; like wild mustangs and tall mountains where a man could breathe clear clean air. Looking back, most of my life had been spent dreaming.

I started in to cuss Cole for saddling me with a job like that. Cleave pulled a shocked face. 'Never heard a preacher use words like them before, did you, Cleave? Don't reckon he'll hang on to that job for long.'

Small grins appearing on their faces told me I

had been taken in. Joining in their laughter helped relieve some of the tension building up in me, but I knew it wouldn't last. The next night would be the longest I'd ever known, even longer than the one spent waiting for the men from the trading post to catch up to me. There had been a small hope then that the men would miss my trail or lose me in the dark. But there was no hiding from the Utes.

Dawn was a long time coming, playing peek a boo over the horizon before daring to show its face. I must have slept some because Cleave and Cole were already up and about, giving orders and making sure that the men chosen to give the alarm and hold back in the attack were ready. Seemed like they had added to my plan during the night. A fresh-dug mound of earth surrounded a shallow grave. The idea of a prayer meeting had turned into a burial. I just hoped that none of us would have need of that grave.

Someone, I didn't know who, had been nominated to play the role of the corpse and was already wrapped in a blanket at graveside. Leastways, I hoped it was someone play-acting. He sure wasn't moving about any.

A preacher man I hadn't known about started to speak fine words over the man in the blanket. Don't know if he really knew the deceased or not but he was talking like he had lost a brother. I

91

wondered if the corpse was smiling and feeling proud of himself. Weren't too many folks who got to listen to their own funeral service. I just hoped he would get a chance to hear it all. He didn't. The man closest to us whispered a warning and we all headed for the nearest wagon. I had never seen so many folks move so fast but none of them beat me. I was first to hit the dirt near my chosen position, scooping up my rifle as I did so. Seemed to be more like a thousand Indians than the forty or fifty Cleave and Cole had tallied and all of them seemed to be heading right at me. My first shot winged a Ute, not the one I was aiming at, but I wasn't about to admit that to nobody.

Cole had taught me better than that. I needed to stop my hand shaking or I was likely to shoot one of my own men. The coolness swept over me. They weren't men out there any more. They were targets, things without faces or any kind of identity. My second shot took a chunk of flesh out of a Ute and he veered away.

The steady fire from the wagon train was taking its toll. Most of the men with me were farmers but I had overlooked the fact that many of the men had also fought in the war and learned to use a gun against their fellow whites. The attack was starting to break up and I knew there would be no other. One Brave more daring than the rest, maybe he had something to prove, was leading the charge. My shot took him down.

It was the last straw. The rest of the Utes retreated to a safe distance. Could I be wrong? Could they be re-grouping for another attack? Somehow I didn't think so. I could read defeat in the slump of their shoulders. The others were reading it, too. Brinkley and one of his pals were heading towards the last man I had dropped, knives in their hands. I was but a few steps behind him when he stooped at the side of the Ute. Brinkley's knife flashed once in the sunlight but the cocking of my six-gun stopped him in his actions.

'Just one inch further, Brinkley, and I'll kill you.'

He turned slowly. 'It's OK, kid. I was going to make you a present of his scalp anyhow. Didn't think you had the stomach or the know-how to do it yourself.'

I drove my left hand into his grinning face with all the power I could muster. It was enough. Blood spouted from his broken nose. 'Get back to the train, and from here on in keep well out of my way, you and your friends.'

Mumbling something, he left supported by his friend. I looked down at the Indian, not wanting to look death in the face but compelled to. Dark eyes looked up at me. Life still existed there but it was ebbing fast. He was young, younger than me even, only a boy. He had no business dying in battle. His hand reached for the coup stick near his side. Out of his reach, but I nudged it closer to him with my foot. For some reason that coup stick was important to him.

His hand closed around it and he tried to lift it but his strength was fading fast. Now I finally understood what it was he needed to do. I knelt at his side, taking a chance. I doubted that he had strength enough left in him to do me much harm with that stick. Gently, the stick touched my shoulder. He smiled, and died.

I wasn't even aware of any others nearby until I felt Cleave touch me. 'You've done all you can do for him, Jim. I'm proud of you.'

'Why, because I killed a man?' I snapped angrily. The Utes were no longer just targets. They had faces, feelings, families, too. Someone would be mourning the death of their son tonight, and I was the one who had taken that life from them.'

'No, Jim,' Cleave said softly. 'I'm proud of you because you accepted him as just another human being. The colour of his skin makes no difference to you. It gives me some hope for the human race, after all. You helped him die with pride. He died thanking you.'

I turned away from him, shamed by the tears in my eyes. 'He was only a boy. I didn't know what he was doing. For some reason he wanted to touch me with that damned stick.'

'He was counting coup, Jim, probably his first. Any Indian can take scalps but it takes the bravest of all the warriors to touch an armed enemy with a coup stick. It's the greatest honour they can achieve. His name will live among the Utes now.'

He stopped talking to watch the rest of the Utes approach slowly, trying to read their intent. His voice rose loud and clear: 'They're coming in to pick up their dead and wounded. It's over. Kill any man who tries to stop them, Cole.'

'Already got my gun on Brinkley,' Cole answered cheerfully. 'Won't need much of an excuse to pull the trigger. We got no use for him now, have we?'

'None at all,' Cleave said. 'We are going to have to stay here, Jim. Show our good faith in them. Think you are up to it?' He didn't wait for an answer. 'Yeah, you're up to it. You've only got one thing left to prove, but that may prove to be the toughest of all.'

I wondered what he was talking about but there was no time to ask. The Utes were closing about us, led by an elderly warrior I guessed was Red Wolf. He had the bearing of a chief.

He reined his paint pony to a halt before us, his eyes looking down sadly at the young brave near my feet. 'The young one has tears in his eyes for the death of my son. Why should this be?'

'Because he cares,' Cleave said. 'A man's life is important to him, and the colour of his skin matters nothing. Your son was a brave warrior.'

Red Wolf nodded. 'I saw what the young one did for my son, One-arm. It was a good thing. My son will now ride a warrior's pony in the life beyond this one. Some day perhaps the young one and my son will meet again and ride warrior ponies together. This, too, will be a good thing.'

He watched two of his braves load his son's body onto a horse before wheeling his horse and riding away. In minutes the land was silent again, and it was as if nothing had ever happened there. Only the blood-stained grass served as a reminder.

I had had my first taste of killing and it was a bitter taste, but I would have that taste in my mouth again when I came face to face with Jefferson Wilde.

Nine

Red Wolf's words had struck more deeply than he would ever know. I had killed his son but there had been no anger in him, no thought of revenge. He had accepted the fact that his son had died bravely in battle. I couldn't accept it that easily. His son's face would stay with me for a long time.

Cleave had my sorrel saddled for me when I finally got back to the wagons. 'I thought we'd move on a while, get a few miles away from here before we settle down again. I want you to ride flank. Thought you needed some time on your own. It's the way I felt the first time I killed a man.'

'Did it get any easier for you?' The words had left my mouth before I was aware of even thinking them. There was an edge to my words that he didn't like.

'Too damned easy, boy,' he snapped. 'The only way to beat it is to isolate yourself from it. Gets

97

that way with a lot of life's problems. You learn to shut yourself off. The first day is the hardest but then you find out that you have pushed it back so far that it is no longer a part of your life. It ceases to exist then.'

He was talking about something other than killing but I didn't know what the something was. Probably never would. Didn't matter much anyhow. Other than our shared interest in wanting Jefferson Wilde dead we had nothing in common.

Having the pup along helped take my mind off things as I rode out alone. When he got tired of exploring I leaned from the saddle to scoop him up. I had caught a glimpse of Lindy watching me as I rode out. She gave my mind another path to follow. She deserved better than me but avoiding her might not be the right answer. That could only make a woman like her more determined. Women's minds worked different from a man's.

Hearing my name called, I turned to watch her riding up on Cleave's horse. Maybe this was his idea of another joke. His last attempt at humour had me joining in the laughter, but there was nothing funny in this one.

'What are you doing out here?'

'Mr Devlin – Cleave thought you were in need of some company. He loaned me his horse.'

'Didn't think you were a horse thief,' I grunted.

'Get back to the wagons.'

'Cleave thinks it's quite safe out here for me, and I trust his judgement.'

'Wasn't thinking of our safety. I was thinking of my own,' I said.

Her smile threw me. 'I've got you worried, haven't I, Jim Wilde? That's a good sign. It means you are interested. Not that you have any hope of escaping from me anyway. I always get what I want. We could go on playing this silly game of yours, and perhaps you'll win. But I'd remind you that you are not the only player in the game.'

I wished I knew what she was talking about. She was picking up Cleave and Cole's habit of talking around me like I wasn't even there.

'Hope they play the game better than me,' I said sourly, wondering if it was Cleave's idea for her to come out here on her own. Either way I was in no mood for company right now.

'Let's just say that they may have more to offer. Oscar Berger's father is quite a successful business man, and Oscar is his only heir. A woman should always consider her future.'

I hadn't known his name until now but I knew who she meant. I had seen him making cow-eyes at her last night when we had sat down to eat at the Blaine wagon. He hadn't liked me, or the attention Lindy had been paying me, but he was no threat. Fact was, Oscar looked like he was ninety cents short of a dollar. I held back my laughter and put a serious face on.

'Struck me as someone who would make his mark some day,' I said. It would probably be an X in place of his signature but I wasn't about to say that. 'Better snap him up before someone else does. Guess there'll be a lot of girls in Oregon ready to take up with him.'

Her eyes were suddenly angry. 'You're making fun of me, Jim Wilde, but I'll have the last laugh. I promise you.'

'I'll start saving up for a wedding present,' I told her. 'Hope I get an invite. Been a long time since I was at a wedding.'

A smile suddenly appeared from nowhere. 'Oh, you'll be at this one, I guarantee you. It couldn't take place without you.'

Laughing loudly, she wheeled Cleave's horse and rode away. I was in real trouble, the kind that every man in his right mind wants to avoid. If she had her way, Oscar was going to be one very disappointed man. Wouldn't be too happy myself. My thoughts were kind of confused. I had never had a girl come on to me that way before. I had taken over first place in her affections from Oscar but that was sure as hell no compliment. A coon dog could have taken over from him.

Long before dark the wagons came to a stop and I headed back. I was in need of a coffee, but determined not to join the Blaines for supper tonight. The best way to solve the problems of Lindy Blaine would be for Cole, Cleave and me to go our separate way, but they would never agree to that. There were still many dangers to be faced and the plain fact was that they couldn't make it without our help. Besides, I would never rest easy knowing that Brinkley and his pals were back in charge of the train.

He was watching me, his eyes burning with hate, as I unsaddled and rubbed down the sorrel before feeding him. If Cole and Cleave hadn't been along there was a good chance they would have found me one morning with my throat cut. I was getting nasty looks from Oscar now, too, and my ears were starting to burn a little, but I just couldn't take him seriously. Somehow I couldn't see Oscar and me facing each other on a duelling ground.

Cleave had also noticed the looks I was getting as he handed me the coffee mug with my initials scratched on it. 'You sure seem to be making yourself popular around here.'

'You didn't help much by loaning her your horse,' I grunted back.

'I told you I wanted to be alone.'

'I figured you had been alone long enough. Thought you needed something else to think about. It worked, didn't it? She took your mind off your problem.'

'Yeah, and gave me a bigger one. And that one ain't going to go away so easy. She's making plans for me that I don't want no part of.'

He let a slight grin touch his face. 'Could be the making of you. Some men just aren't complete without a woman. It depends upon making the right choice, if we've got any real choice in the matter. A bad woman can kill a man as surely as a bullet, but it takes a lot longer to do it.'

'Cleave Devlin, authority on women,' I said. 'Didn't even know that you knew any women.'

'I've known women, kid, good, bad and indifferent. Some will suck the life-blood from a man and leave him empty, but they are devious enough to hide that fact until it's too late. Then there is the other kind.'

His voice had softened on the last sentence, making me curious. It seemed like Cleave was talking about one particular woman, and I needed to know more about her. Why, I didn't know. Maybe it was the tender far-away look in his eyes.

'What kind?' I asked quietly.

'The kind that makes it all worthwhile, Jim. The kind that gives your life meaning. I knew someone like that once. I loved her so much it hurt each time I looked at her, but not as much as it hurt when I looked at myself and knew she was deserving of better than me. Funny thing was she never thought that way. She loved me and that was all that happened.'

'What happened to her?'

'She became part of my past. Fate dealt me the wrong hand but I had to play it the best way I knew how. I had to decide what was best for her. I guess, like a million men before me, I made the wrong decision.'

He stretched, signalling the end of the conversation, but there were still questions that I wanted to ask. For a long time Cleave had tried to hide himself in a bottle. Because of her? Could parting from a woman really hurt that much? Love had almost destroyed him but it was hate that was dragging him back again – hate for a man named Jefferson Wilde.

In the past day or two I had been getting a look at the kind of man Cleave Devlin once was, and I was starting to like what I was seeing. But there were still depths to Devlin that no one was allowed to reach. Funny thing was I found it hard to believe Cleave capable of the hate that he was showing to get back at Jefferson Wilde. Did it have something to do with the woman Cleave had once, still, loved and lost?

I wondered if Cole had ever felt that way about a woman. It seemed unlikely; Cole was the foot-loose type with no thoughts of settling down. But there was a mystery about him that I hadn't yet fathomed. Truth was, it had been playing on my mind for a while now but I hadn't wanted to face up to it.

He had been there when I had need of him to lead me away from Kelp and his men, to help me against the men from the trading post. As I recalled now, there hadn't been too many questions asked when we first met. He had known about Jefferson Wilde and the men on my trail. Most other men would have ridden away from that kind of trouble, but not Cole Masters. He had stepped in like it was his fight, too.

The footprints on the knoll were coming back to mind, too. They hadn't belonged to Kelp or any of his men, but they could have belonged to Cole Masters. It could be that Cole Masters had known who I was all along and was using me to get to Jefferson Wilde. I was the means to an end, providing the wagon and money to enable him to reach the man he wanted.

'Where's Cole?' I asked, trying to keep my voice even.

Still something in my tone made Cleave suspicious. He shrugged. 'Who knows? Only sure thing about Cole is that he'll turn up when the smell of cooking reaches him. Seems to me that you've got something in mind, kid, but if I was you I'd forget it. Only known one man better with a gun than Cole Masters, and it ain't you. Doubt that he'll kill you, but he'll sure make you look foolish.'

'There are some things I need to know. I think Cole can give me the answers.'

'Don't reckon Cole will balk at answering a few questions, just so they are asked in the right way. But it might be best if you leave your gun in the wagon.'

I wasn't about to heed his advice. The more I was thinking on it the more convinced I became that I was right. Cole Masters knew a lot more than he had told. It could be that he was part of Kelp's outfit. For all I knew, he could be out there right now talking to Kelp.

My anger had reached boiling point when he finally hove into view. There was barely time for him to unsaddle his mount before he found me facing him.

'You've lied to me all along, haven't you? You knew about Kelp and his men before I did. They were your footprints I found on the knoll each morning.'

If I expected him to be taken aback I was disappointed.

'No, boy. I haven't lied to you. Just refused to tell you all the truth is all. Sure, I knew who you were, and I knew about Kelp. If you hadn't got out of that town on your own I'd have had to step in to help you. But you made it out on your own, using more intelligence than I gave you credit for. As for me visiting your mama's grave, that was a personal thing – something I needed to do. I've been watching you on and off for a couple of years now, but you weren't aware of it.'

'You've been using me ... using me to get to Jefferson Wilde.'

'That's right, boy. Just as you've been using me for the same purpose. We both needed to get to Jeff Wilde, and my best way was to use you. I didn't know any other way to do it, and it worked. I'm not on Kelp's side, if that's what's bothering you.'

Confusion clouded my mind. I was lost again. I had expected Cole to deny my accusations, but he hadn't. The truth seemed to be slipping away from me again.

'Who are you?' I asked, hardly able to hear my own voice.

'Cole Masters. It's the name I was born with, never saw any reason to change it. Why was I up on the knoll? That is your next question, isn't it? I met your ma once, a long time ago, and fell in love with her. But she was already married, and there could never be any room for any other man in her life. I wanted to tell her all the things I thought she needed to know, but I couldn't until she was dead.

'I liked to spend time up there on the knoll. Liked to talk to her. Had the feeling she was hearing every word I said.'

I knew what he meant. I had always had that feeling, too. 'She's the reason you want Jeff Wilde dead? She wouldn't like that.'

'It's the same reason you've got, isn't it, Jim?

Ten

Knowing why Cole Masters wanted Jefferson Wilde dead didn't help much. We shared the same reason and the same burden of guilt. That guilt seemed to be getting heavier with each foot along the trail to Oregon. Cole had said something else too; something about owing it to a friend to meet up with Jeff Wilde. He hadn't added anything to that remark, just leaving it hanging in the air.

After my talk with Cole I was in no mood for company and went straight to my wagon. A little before dusk I heard a knock on the tailgate of the wagon and looked out to find Lindy waiting there with a plate of food.

'Ma sent this over. She thinks you need some filling out. I don't think she would take it too kindly if you refused.'

I climbed down. Given that Mrs Blaine had taken the trouble to cook up a meal for me I could hardly refuse. Still, the thought that she might be a confederate in her daughter's scheme to snare me crossed my mind.

'I can leave if you want me to,' Lindy said. 'Cole said he didn't think you wanted company tonight. Are you sick?'

Her concern touched me. The only side I had seen of Lindy Blaine before was that of a young, flighty girl with no thought of anyone else in her mind.

I shook my head. 'No, I'm not sick, although a lot of people would consider it to be a kind of sickness. Maybe they are right. I don't want you to leave. I want you to stay. Please.'

Her radiant smile warmed me. My defences were down and she needed to take advantage of it. Unlike Cole, I had known what Lindy Blaine's motive was from the first time we had set eyes upon each other.

'Would you like to talk about it?' she asked gently, concern plain in her face. 'Sometimes it helps.'

I wasn't sure that I could put it into words. Being betrayed hurt. I had come to depend upon Cole Masters as a friend, but that was ended now. He had lied to me, or evaded the truth, in his effort to get me to help him to reach Jefferson Wilde. Sure he had saved my life along the way, but that had served his purpose, too. My being dead wouldn't help him in his search at all.

From what little I knew of Jefferson Wilde he could disappear at will. Already years had passed since he had been seen or heard of. There was no guarantee that mention of my name would bring Jeff Wilde out of hiding, but Cole would figure the odds to be in our favour.

My continued silence was getting to her as she watched the conflict on my face.

'It's something I don't know if I can share with you yet, Lindy.'

'Is ... is that bad?'

'I have to kill a man. Cleave and Cole are helping me to find him.'

'Who is he?'

'Jefferson Wilde. My father. Leastways, that's probably how he considers himself. I don't recall ever thinking of him that way. He deserted my mother and me when I was about eight years old. Left her to work her life away in a dry-dirt farm. Until I sold that farm neither of us had a dollar to call our own. She wouldn't sell. The farm was her home – it was the place Jefferson Wilde was coming back to. But he never did.

'It isn't nice to watch someone die inch by inch, but that's the way it happened with Ma. I watched the life go from her eyes first. Every time someone appeared on the horizon those eyes of hers would light up. She was always disappointed and another spark of life would disappear. When hope

111

dies the body follows soon after. Jefferson Wilde killed her as sure as if he put a gun to her head.'

She was quiet for a moment, her hand reaching out to touch my shoulder gently. 'I could tell you that what you are thinking of doing is wrong, Jim, but you already know that, don't you? You'll have to live with it after you kill him. Can you do that?'

It wasn't that cut and dried. Jeff Wilde would be a hard man to kill. The fact that I was his own flesh and blood wouldn't mean a thing to him. Cole had told me that Jeff Wilde was the fastest man he had ever known with a gun.

'If I don't kill him someone else will. There are a lot of men waiting in line for a chance at Jefferson Wilde. Two of those men are riding along with me. They are hoping I can flush him out. Either way, I'll be responsible for his death.'

My words shocked her. 'You hired two men to help you hunt down and kill your own father?'

Put like that it was a fact and I couldn't hide from it. I had known Cole and Cleave's intentions before we left Leeway, but it had made no difference. I wasn't paying them wages as such, but that was a moot point. Without my money to buy supplies and a wagon they could never have left Leeway. Maybe deep in my mind I had wanted them to do my killing for me.

The horror was still in her eyes as she looked at me, no longer liking what she was seeing. 'Cleave and Cole don't strike me as manhunters. Why would they want to kill your father?'

I shrugged, avoiding her eyes. 'Never asked. They got their reasons, and I've got mine. Can't afford the time to ask every man why he wants Jefferson Wilde dead. There are at least five others that I know of who want the same thing. The only person I've ever known to speak a kind word of him was my ma, and she had no reason to.'

I busied my hands and mind with the rolling of a smoke before speaking again. 'You know how it is with me now. I thought you had the right to know about me before things got too involved. I don't like myself much, so there's no reason why anyone else should.'

She reached across to kiss me gently on the cheek. 'A lot of things can happen between now and then. Perhaps your father is feeling the same sense of guilt that you are now living with. You are growing inside all the time. And you now know what it is like to kill a man. Those things do make a difference. Whatever you decide I know it will be the right thing. I've got more faith in you than you have in yourself at the moment.'

Lindy got to her feet at the break-up of the big talk near her wagon. Seemed to me that Brinkley and her father had been having most of the say over there but we were too far away to hear the words.

Her kiss still burned on my cheek as I watched her walk away. There had been doubts about me baring my soul to her that way, but I was feeling pretty good about it now. I was no longer alone, unable to share my deepest fears and thoughts with another. Lindy had shared her strength with me, let me know I was no longer alone, that she would always stand by me. She had understood my feelings after killing the young Ute, known the torment inside me. Those were things that meant a lot to me in ways I couldn't yet put words to.

Cleave barely glanced at me as he hunkered over the coffee pot. There was no sign of Cole Masters, hadn't been for hours.

'Where is he?' I asked bluntly. As far as I was concerned I was Cole Masters' employer and he was answerable to me.

Cleave shrugged. 'Cole? I guess he's wherever he wants to be. I've got no loop on him. He goes where he wants, does what he wants. Always been that way with him.'

'How long have you know him?'

Cleave studied me for a long time before answering. 'Know your enemy, is that it, kid? You're learning, but you're not seeing straight. Cole's not your enemy. You're thinking like a kid again. If he was your enemy he wouldn't have brought you to Leeway. That's about the only mistake I've ever known him make.'

He was talking in riddles again, and again I wasn't about to get any explanation from him. 'I asked you a question: How long have you known him?'

'Since the war. He got the fool notion that he owes me and he's been keeping tabs on me ever since. He never liked what I was doing to myself and resolved to give me back my self-respect. Can't say I like his way of doing it though. Cole's a good man but he's got his own way of doing things, and they can sometimes get a little rough. And sometimes he doesn't think too far ahead, but that's something I'll have to handle when the time comes.'

In his own way Cleave was as big a puzzle as Cole Masters. Would the pieces ever come together? Somehow, I was getting the feeling that I was the one holding those pieces apart. But how?

'Whatever your differences are with Cole, I want them settled,' Cleave continued. 'They held a meeting over by the Blaine wagon tonight, elected me the new wagon boss. I'll need all the help I can get. You and Cole will be my new scouts. He'll teach you all you need to know, if you are big enough to learn from him.'

So that was why Brinkley had been doing so much air-chomping over there tonight. He had just lost his job and wasn't too happy about it. That was just one more reason to hate Cleave Devlin. He would have to watch his back from here on in. Something about Brinkley had irked me ever since I had first set eyes upon him. Maybe it had something to do with that sly smile he had on his face most times; it said he had a secret that he wasn't about to share with us. Or maybe it had something to do with the fact that he had chosen a path away from the Oregon trail and put a lot of lives in danger. Either way, Brinkley was a man who would need watching.

'When a man stops learning he stops growing,' I said quietly. 'I figure I've still got a lot of growing to do.'

He nodded, satisfied. Maybe there was hope for me, after all. 'Would have invited you to the election, but you had other things on your mind at the time. Lindy would have had me by the throat if I had tried to take you away from her then.'

I let a quiet grin slip by. 'Know what you mean. To tell the truth she scares the hell out of me, too.'

My grin relieved him. 'Felt that way myself, a long time ago. It's the kind of feeling that you never want to leave you. She becomes your only reason for being alive.'

'What was she like, Cleave?' I asked softly, sensing his need to put into words how he felt about her. Maybe I needed those words too, to

116

fully understand my own feelings about Lindy.

'Too good for the likes of me, kid. The best thing I ever did for her was walk away. Probably the hardest thing I ever did, too, but that's how it had to be. I couldn't let her see what I had become.'

His words were cut off by the arrival of Cole Masters. He was keeping a cautious eye on me as he dismounted slowly, but I wasn't his only cause for concern. I had ridden with him long enough to know that. His eyes narrowed and he watched me as I climbed uncertainly to my feet.

'Looks like things haven't been too easy for you out there. I'll take care of your horse while you get some food inside you. They're keeping something hot for you over at the Blaines'.'

'Now that is a relief,' he said, letting his tension ease out through his grin. 'I was afraid I'd have to face up to your cooking again.'

That wasn't the only thing he was afraid of, but he wouldn't get it said until after he ate. More trouble was heading our way, and I was glad to have Cole Masters back on my side.

Eleven

Cole had collected his food from the Blaines' wagon and finished eating by the time I returned from rubbing down, feeding and picketing his horse. Cleave had already parted with the information that he was the new wagon boss.

'Couldn't have made a better choice myself,' Cole told him. 'I guess I make all my reports to you now.'

'As my chief scout you do,' Cleave said. 'You can start with whatever is bothering you now.'

'Something and nothing,' Cole shrugged. 'Just a feeling I got like someone's following us, but don't want us to know about it.'

'Utes?'

'Don't feel like Indians. Feels more like white men.' He caught the look on my face and shook his head. 'Too soon for Kelp to be this close to us. He's coming – we can bet on that – but it isn't him, yet.'

'Who else would be out there?' I asked. 'Maybe you are just getting edgy.'

'I'm going to stay that way until I find out for sure,' Cole said. He gave Cleave a pointed look. 'You thinking what I'm thinking?'

'Yeah, and I hope we're both wrong.' He threw the dregs of his coffee into the fire and straightened up. 'Think I'll take a little walk around, get to know a few more people. We need to know how many men we can rely on.'

There was a proud glint in Cole's eyes as he watched Cleave walk away with a new set to his shoulders. 'He's walking tall again. I've waited a long time for that, and most of it is down to you. You helped give him back his pride and his belief in himself as a man.'

How I had managed that I didn't know. Of course, I had taken note of Cleave's struggle with himself ever since we had left Leeway, but it had been a lone battle. There was nothing Cole or I could do to aid him. Cleave's fight wasn't over yet, but his hands had stopped shaking and his eyes were clear again.

'I didn't do nothing,' I said. 'Hell, I didn't even know he existed until you led me to him. Even then I was against bringing him along with us. Remember? Have to admit I was wrong. Maybe I should tell him that.'

'You already have in many ways. You took him

at his word, never questioned his worth as a man.
Never even went looking for any bottles he might
have brought along. Fact is, I don't think it even
crossed your mind. Been a long, long time since
anyone showed that much faith in Cleave Devlin.
That means a lot to him.'

'What makes a man want to hide inside a
bottle, Cole?' Not being much of a drinker myself
it was hard to understand why anyone would
want to hide from life that way.

'Lots of reasons. Some men just develop a taste
for it. With someone like Cleave it goes a lot
deeper. He didn't want to face himself again, until
he had to. But it isn't over for him yet. His biggest
fight is yet to come. I don't know if he can win that
one.'

His eyes had a faraway look as if he was talking
to himself, and maybe he was. It seemed like
every time I felt I was getting close to Cole or
Cleave they slipped away again, leaving me to
flounder.

Looked like the conversation was ended as Cole
rolled a cigarette, his face thoughtful. Whatever
those thoughts were he hadn't yet decided to
share them with me. His eyes avoided mine as he
lit the smoke with a twig from the fire.

'Ten years is a long time for a man to be lost,
Jim. After a while he starts to wonder if there is
any road back. Cleave was an officer in the Union

Army when I first met him. Even then the blood and carnage of the war had taken its toll. A lot of men had died under him, but their voices and faces still lived inside him. Even then guilt was riding him with long-rowelled spurs.

'The place where we met didn't even have a name but close on a hundred bodies littered the field. I can still see his face coming towards me, empty, his eyes dead as if he couldn't believe that humans could create such mayhem on each other. The mist was thick that morning, and I was scared and all because his uniform was a different colour to mine.

'I was a Johnny Reb, wounded and unarmed. He was a Blue Belly. I could see the blood on his left arm and knew he was hurt too, but he had a gun. He stood over me, and for the first time I saw the flicker of life in his eyes. I was but a couple of years younger than him, but he called me kid as he leaned over me. I guess being in command ages a man pretty quick. I still don't know how he got me over his shoulder, but he did it. It took the best part of a week for him to get me to the nearest field hospital. Most of that time was spent hiding me from his own men. Tempers were running pretty high and any man in a grey uniform was likely to get shot out of hand. Cleave Devlin wasn't about to take that chance.

'He saved my life by getting me to the hospital,

but it was too late to do anything about his own arm. Kind of a miracle that he got me there at all. As soon as I was well enough they transferred me to a prison camp. Cleave was moved to a real hospital. The war ended without him even being aware of it. I can't imagine what kind of hell he went through with all that pain. The poison had spread through his whole body. By the time he left that hospital he was living in the twilight world of a morphine addict.

'There is no reality in that world. He had no home, no previous life, no family. His only memory was that of a Grey Belly he had carried from a battlefield, but I was there to remind him of that. As soon as the war ended and I had turned over my sabre I headed back to find Cleave. I owed him. As soon as Cleave realized what was happening to him, he fought back. The war had been over for two years by the time he beat the addiction. But he couldn't beat the demons inside his own head.

'He was no longer a man. He was nothing more than a number on the hospital records. He couldn't plough a field any more, use a rifle, or do any number of things he had just taken for granted before. Cleave Devlin had been one hell of a man then. He couldn't live with being anything less. Somewhere along the line, he discovered that he could hide from reality by climbing into a bottle. The demons had happy faces then.'

It was a story that I hadn't liked hearing, but it seemed that I had played some small part in giving Cleave back his life and I was grateful for that. He was a man again, in control of his own mind and destiny. It said a lot about Cole Masters, too. He had gone far beyond repaying a debt. His life had been dedicated to helping a friend regain his lost dignity.

Of course, there had been times when Cole had left Cleave alone – there had to be. But it was a sure thing that Cole had left him well cared-for when he left. It hadn't been chance when Cole had come across me and he had used it not only to his advantage, but also to that of his friend. I could hardly blame him for that. It had worked out to my advantage, too. I was proud to know these men.

A sudden grin touched Cole's face and he nodded to one of the wagons. 'Seems your rival is on the prowl. Hardly mistake me for Lindy, can he?'

I caught glimpse of Oscar retreating back into the shadows. Seemed like he was keeping an eye on me all the time from here on in. As yet, I hadn't spoken to him at all. Fact was, I had heard that it was most people's ambition to avoid Oscar.

'Only human I ever know that had more turn to his neck than an owl,' Cole said. 'Should have given him to the Utes as a peace offering. Two kinds of men that Indians respect almost as much as a brave warrior. First, there's the kind that simper a lot and spend most of their days doing fancy needlework. And then there's the kind that – how shall I put it – only got one foot in the saddle?'

I burst out laughing. 'Oscar probably qualifies on both counts.'

Oscar's head reappeared from behind a wagon again, looking daggers in my direction, and Cole joined in the laughter. 'Yeah, I can just about see him as a dressmaker.'

I had a vision of Oscar sewing a dress for Lindy, but the thought that it could be a wedding dress cut short my grin. I knew that I would never find anything better than Lindy in my life, but I wasn't yet ready to put my neck in that noose. I still had a job to do.

The simmering heat of the desert hurt my eyes as we halted on the rim overlooking it. With the aid of Cleave's field glasses I could already see the bleached bones of oxen, mules, horses, that had failed in their attempt to reach the other side. Doubtless there were the bones of people out there, too. Discarded furniture marked the path those people had chosen to cross – a land that looked to me like the remnants of hell. I wondered how many of those wagons had made it. Most hadn't. I could see the carcasses.

Cleave shook his head sadly. 'The gates of hell are always open for a fool, Jim. No one in their right mind would even think about crossing this place before dark. We'll rest up for a day or two, make sure every animal is in top condition before we set out.'

We had ridden on ahead on horseback, leaving Cole in charge of our wagon. 'No other way?' I asked.

'Mountains either side of the desert, and land too rugged for wagons to cross. I'm afraid this is the only way. Make sure you've got a heavy coat to hand when we make the crossing.'

I looked at him, wondering what the punchline of his joke was. That sun was hot enough to blister the hide of an alligator. 'Fur-lined gloves, too?' I asked.

'OK, kid. Find out the hard way.'

I shrugged. Maybe age was catching up to Cleave and he was starting to feel the cold. 'Thought about what you are going to do after we get to Oregon, Cleave?'

'After we kill Jefferson Wilde, you mean?'

I didn't like the way he put it into words. I had pushed Jeff Wilde far back into my mind. It was the only way I could live with it. 'Yeah,' I said. 'After we kill him.'

126

He shrugged. 'Haven't thought too much about it. Maybe I'll chase mustangs for a while. Build up a herd that way. Horses are good people. Treat them right and they'll stand by you.'

'Can't see you busting horses, Cleave. That's a job for a younger man.'

'And one with two good arms, huh, kid? Wasn't thinking about slapping leather on them and just stepping into the saddle. There are easier ways of doing things. My way it might take a month or six months to break a horse, but there'll be no fear or cruelty involved. But by the end of that time we'll be friends, and we'll both have trust on our side.'

That would be something to see. Knowing Cleave he had already worked out a plan to become friends with the animals he chose. I had already noticed that he never passed a horse, dog or the two cats we had aboard the wagon train without knowing their names and talking to them. It had been easy to spot because I had me the same habit. In our own peculiar way we each felt a need to communicate and become friends with each animal we saw. Doubted that it would work with a grizzly bear or cougar though.

Cole had disappeared after supper last night again and returned after midnight to make his report to Cleave. I didn't need to be told that those men were still on our trail. Who they were and what they wanted, I didn't know. All I could be sure of was they were trouble, the kind that neither Cleave or Cole wanted.

Twelve

There was no longer time to think about the men coming along behind us as we set off as soon as the sun dipped below the far-off mountains. Those mountains looked good to me. I had me a real need to touch them. Cleave had offered me some good advice. I should have paid heed, but it was hard to believe that any land so hot by day could get so cold as soon as the sun disappeared.

Cleave said nothing as I climbed into the wagon in search of my coat, but there was a wry glint in his eye. The pup was reluctant to part with my coat but gave it up after a struggle.

The ghosts of the desert voiced their protests on the wind as we trundled onward, most of us walking to help conserve the strength of our animals. By Cleave's reckoning, it would take us best part of two days to cross this forsaken land. Most of our travelling would be done at night. Before sun-up, we stopped to rig up shelters to protect us from the sun's blazing rays. The horses were bunched together in the shade of the wagons, their heads drooping.

I had never felt such strength-sapping heat. Even the chore of watering the horses, little and often, drained me. Those mountains seemed to be moving away from us each time I looked in their direction. We could hardly wait for the sun to sink again. The chill of the night seemed like the breath of God after the heat. What restless sleep I had during the day was tormented by visions of cold mountain streams.

There was no stopping this time when the sun lifted its head into the skies again, but nobody minded. Even the horses felt the pull of the mountains, setting to their work with a fresh vigour, eager to leave this sun-seared land far behind. Yet there was a strange beauty to the desert that I liked. I had heard the siren song that called many men back to its bosom.

It was a land that asked for and gave no quarter. The animals that dwelled within it had learned to accept and adapt to its ways. Most men lacked that much sense. They fought against a land that couldn't be beaten; they lost by denying it the respect it deserved. My respect for it was born out of fear, but we would both accept that.

The kind of stream that had tortured my sleep

awaited us, deep and cold with sweet-tasting, swift-running water. There wasn't a man, woman or child among us who wasn't eager to get into that water. As soon as the chores were taken care of, the horses watered, men and women went their separate ways to bathe and enjoy the cool water. I was reminded of a kids' swimming hole and all the excitement it built up.

Cole and I stayed behind to watch the wagon, mostly in case a bear or a cougar wandered along. Bears were our biggest fear. Seemed like they could smell food from a mile off. I had never seen a bear but I'd heard the tales. They were fiesty creatures with a talent for destruction and getting into mischief. Not much different from kids, come to think on it.

There were other things on my mind, too. Using Cleave's field glasses, I checked our back trail as best I could, but there was nothing to see out there in that savage land – not even sign of our own passage. It was hard to believe that a desert could live so close to water and not be touched by it.

'You're looking in the wrong direction, kid,' Cole said. 'They're ahead of us now. Passed by us about four nights ago. It's part of their plan. Wouldn't do to alert us by letting us think they've been following us. But they're not ready to hit us yet. The closer we get to their base of operations the easier it is for them.'

'Who are they? What do they want with us?'

'Anything that will bring in a dollar, kid. Rawhiders aren't too fussy how they make their dollar. If you've still got any qualms about killing a man I want you to forget them before we meet up with the bunch that's waiting for us. You are pretty good with that gun now. Shoot first, shoot fast, and shoot to kill. That's the best advice I can give you.'

'We're talking about men,' I reminded him.

'No, Jim. We're talking about rawhiders. They lost any right to call themselves men a long time ago, about the same time they lost the right to go on living. You've got a price on your head the same as the rest of us and you don't even know it. Hat? Maybe four, five dollars. Coat? About the same, providing there aren't too many bullet-holes in it. Your guns, belt, horse, saddle, boots, all mean money to a rawhider. That's all he sees. But the real value lies down there in the stream. No way of knowing how much a woman is worth to a rawhider.

'Any kind of female – age don't matter – is worth a lot of money in this country. There's always a lonely prospector ready to part with his last grain of gold dust to share his life with a woman. Her looks won't bother him too much, and he won't ask any questions. Just takes her back with him to some mountain in the middle of nowhere. She might be the lucky one. Someone else might find herself traded off to an Indian for furs or a few ponies. Either way, neither of them gets seen or heard of again.

'All the males are killed. Boys grow into men and could cause trouble later on. Besides, no one wants to buy them. Girls grow into women. Hard to say how many girls and women have disappeared in this country at the hands of raw-hiders.'

I found it hard to believe that such evil existed, but I couldn't deny the hate in Cole's eyes or the venom in his voice. Besides, history was full of evil men. Why should this era be different?

'How ... how will we handle it? We could try losing them.'

'No way we can do that, Jim. Anyhow, Cleave wants them to come to us. He wants them under our guns. When that happens you shoot fast, shoot straight, and don't even think about it.'

'I'm not Cleave's hired gun,' I said coldly. 'If he wants any killing done, let him handle it himself.'

Cole's lips tightened. 'He'll do his share, boy, and he won't lose any sleep over it. But he can't do it alone. We need someone to watch our backs. That was supposed to be your job, but it don't look like you are up to it. Maybe we should get Oscar to do it.'

Cole really knew how to hurt a man. 'If you

133

were that smart you wouldn't let a man get behind you.'

'We've had guns pointed at our backs ever since we joined this train, boy, but you are too dumb to realize it.'

'Am I supposed to understand that?' I asked, feeling the anger rising inside me, but not sure why I should get so het up. The killing of the Ute still rested heavy on my conscience, and now Cole was talking about killing more men as if we would be doing the world some kind of favour. Could be I was just plain scared, though.

It was one thing to kill a nameless, faceless man who was coming at you with the same purpose in mind, but something else to look into a man's eyes and know you are meant to kill him. Cleave would be leading those men into a trap with the sole intent of murdering them. There could be no other word for it.

Cole shook his head sadly. 'I had hopes for you once, boy, but now I'm not so sure. You haven't even learned to ask yourself any questions. Don't you reckon it's kind of strange the rawhiders knew exactly where to find this train? They've been following it for quite a while, since long before we joined up. That put a crimp in someone's plans. A rawhider's usual plan is to wait along a known trail until they find a train to their liking – not too well-guarded and with plenty of women aboard. They couldn't have asked for better than this one.

'Not too many people know about rawhiders, mainly because there are never any witnesses left behind to tell of them after one of the raids. Anyhow, white folk prefer to blame Indians for every massacre that takes place. Maybe their last raid didn't net them the kind of profit they wanted so they changed their method. If they waited in Missouri they could select the best pickings. This was first choice, but they needed a few extra cards up their sleeves to help their plan along. Know what I'm talking about now, Jim?'

I did, but didn't like it. Cole could be wrong in his thinking, but I doubted it. He had been proved right too many times before. We had come across the train way too many times before. We had come across the train way off the usual trails but I hadn't given much thought to it. Brinkley and his friends hadn't struck me as very bright men, so I had just let it go at that. If – and I still didn't like what Cole was hinting at – he was right, our arrival and his dismissal as wagon boss had put a big crimp in his plans.

The sickening part of it was the fact that it would have worked. The wagon train would have been wiped out without a shot being fired in defence.

'We can cut the odds right away,' I said, the

blood rising in me. Brinkley and his men had shared food with these people while plotting their murder.'

Cole shook his head. 'Nope. We've decided just to let them go ahead with their plan. Sorry, kid, but they've all got to die. It's the only way.'

His eyes watched me, waiting for my reaction. I was the weak link in their plan. Cleave and he needed my help but a second's hesitation on my part could prove fatal to all of us.

'Just as long as you leave Brinkley to me,' I said.

'He's yours. We're getting close to their usual stamping grounds so we can expect company in the next few days. Be ready.'

I was ready now. I had seen the way Brinkley and his friends looked at Lindy and some of the other girls and women. Killing every last one of the rawhiders was the only way. Cleave and Cole had accepted that fact. I had to now. A little while ago I would have rebelled at such a thought, but it had to be. These men needed to be killed to make the land safer for those coming behind us. If we failed a lot more people would die at their hands.

'Tell Cleave I won't let him down,' I said softly.

Cole's usual lop-sided grin appeared: 'We never thought you would. You are growing up, Jim, learning to look at things from all sides. Even starting to have second thoughts about a lot of things, I'm thinking.'

'If you're meaning Jefferson Wilde, Cole, you're wrong. He's the reason I'm out here, and I can't forget that. He's got a debt to pay.'

'We all have, Jim. One way or another. I've got a bet to pay too. Much of that debt is paid off now but I've still got a way to go, and I'll kill anyone who tries to stop me paying it off in full.'

He was trying to tell me something, but I didn't know what. All I understood was the thinly veiled warning in his voice. Sometime in the not-too-distant future I would find myself facing up to Cole Masters.

Thirteen

The burden of responsibility rested heavy on my shoulders, and I wondered how long I could carry it. I was alone, Cole and Cleave vanished silently into the dark night at first sight of the approaching strangers. Four of them, not enough to represent a threat, if you didn't know about Brinkley and his friends. I didn't want to be left in command of the camp, didn't feel I could handle it, but they had given me no chance to argue. One mistake from me could ignite the powder keg they had left me with.

Leaning against my wagon, I listened to Dexter, their leader, tell of how they had been on a trail drive but had run out of grub two days before. Spotting our train was a heaven-sent gift they hadn't expected, not the welcome given them by us. The food was the best they had eaten for a long time, and they could hardly refuse the offer to spend the night in our company.

It was a slick, long-practised story, gaining the kind of sympathy they expected as he talked of their urge to get back to their loved ones. His smooth-talking, easy-smiling manner added depth to his tale but I wondered how many people had died after hearing it.

I was looking at Cleave through different eyes. He had accepted command of this train without a second thought, even knowing how many tough decisions he would be forced to make before this journey ended. Yet just a short while ago he had been an empty shell of a man with no future in sight, but fate hadn't finished with Cleave Devlin. There was still another hand to be dealt. Now the futures of a lot of people rested squarely on Cleave's shoulders. I was only starting to learn just how heavy that could be.

Brinkley whispered some back-of-the-hand remark to Dexter and both men glanced in my direction. I was nobody, nothing, so it was a safe bet that Brinkley had noticed that both Cole and Cleave were missing, and that was cause for concern. So far, I had made no attempt to greet the strangers and that needed thinking about, too.

Accompanied by the squint-eyed man and Dexter, Brinkley came towards me. This was the part I didn't like, couldn't handle. Damn Cleave. He should never have left me in this position.

Even sight of the squint-eyed man gave me a sour taste in my belly. The pup didn't like him either, wimpering at his approach, but staying defiantly at my side to defend me.

'Thought I'd introduce Dexter and Cully to Devlin and Masters. Where are they, kid?'

I shrugged. 'Who knows? I didn't ask where they were going and they didn't say. Nice bright moonlit night. Maybe they went fishing or hunting. Never took much to hunting myself. I figure if something wants killing I can sit back and let it come to me.'

Mister Blaine had moved in closer to hear my words and, I guess, assess how I was handling things. He had doubts about these men too, and didn't like the idea of Cleave and Cole being away from camp. A slight nod told me he liked the way I was taking care of things so far.

The pup growled, showing his teeth, as Cully stepped nearer. A boot lifted, ready to take a kick at the pup, but my words stopped him: 'I wouldn't do that if I were you, mister. The last man that abused that pup got himself dead.'

I hadn't killed him but, for some reason, forgot to mention that fact. Still, it worked. Cully and Dexter were having second thoughts about me. They looked at me closely. The tied-down gun at my side didn't belong on no farmer's hip.

The easy smile appeared again on Dexter's face.

'You'll have to excuse Cully, kid. A man gets edgy on a trail drive. Takes him a long time to unwind after. You ever been on a trail drive, kid?'

'Seeing as how I only ever owned one cow, didn't seem like a worthwhile proposition,' I told him. 'Besides, that cow never would drive worth a damn. Always wanted to go in a different direction to me.'

I had confirmed their suspicions about me being a farm boy, but the gun on my hip was still a worry to them. Brinkley couldn't tell them how good I was with a pistol because he'd never seen me use one. But I hadn't acted too bright up till now. Maybe that would give him the advantage they wanted.

'Nice-looking gun, kid,' Dexter said. 'One of the latest model Peacemakers, ain't it? Mind if I take a look at it?'

I grinned. 'That would be a pretty dumb thing for me to do, wouldn't it, mister? Anyhow the man who taught me to use it would have my ears if I did anything as stupid as that. He reckons the only time I should show a man my gun is when I intend it to be his last look.'

That took him back some. Maybe it was hard for him to believe but I wasn't as dumb as I looked. 'Which one taught you, kid, Masters or Devlin?'

'Cole Masters, but he doesn't stack himself that

high. He still reckons he's second best. But I'd sure hate to go up against the man who can beat him.'

I watched Dexter throw an angry glance at Brinkley. He had failed to warn them about Cole Masters but, there again, Brinkley had no way of knowing how fast Cole was with a short gun. All our practising had been done far away from the wagon train. It was too late to back out now. All their plans had been made with just one small change: Cole Masters would have to be the first to die.

'One thing to beat a man to the draw, but something else to pull the trigger on him,' Cully said. 'Figure you are up to that, kid?'

'Got the feeling I'm going to find out before too long,' I answered easily. 'I reckon it will be easier for me to kill some men than others. Just a degree of hate, I guess.'

Movement at the edge of the wagon circle caught my eye, and I was relieved to see Cole Masters come into sight. A quick nod gave me the sign that everything was under control. His grin told me he liked the way I was handling things.

'Got anyone in mind for killing, boy?' Cully asked, his face tight with pent-up anger.

'Well, I reckon you will do for starters,' I grinned. 'Given the nature of your work, I reckon it will be a pleasure to kill you.' I let my grin broaden. 'Guess this is something of a novelty for you; facing a man I mean. If you are depending upon the men you left out there I'm afraid you are going to be disappointed. Right now, I'd say they are holding the gates of hell open for you.'

'That's big talk for a boy on his own. All you got backing you is a bunch of dirt farmers,' Cully snapped. 'I'm going to enjoy killing you, boy.'

'Easy, Cully,' Dexter said, not liking the way things were going. I was too confident. 'Remember we are guests here. It looks like we've out-stayed our welcome. Maybe it's time we moved on.'

'Can't let you do that. Seeing that Cleave and Cole took all that trouble to kill the rest of your men it wouldn't be polite for you to leave without giving them a chance to kill you, too.'

'Those friends of yours should have taught you to keep your mouth shut, boy. Could save you a lot of trouble in the long term.'

His smile had vanished, so I let mine take over. 'They tried, but I guess they just about gave up by now. They taught me a lot of things though. Never even heard of rawhiders until a short while ago. I learned to hate them before I even set eyes on one. Hard for me to even think of them as men any more, so any time you're ready, Squint, you just pull iron. I promised myself that I'd be the one to kill you the first time I saw you.'

Dexter's hand touched Cully, restraining him.

144

Things weren't going according to plan, and I was too cocky by half. I had an ace in the hole that they didn't know about. Brinkley and his friends started to back off as if none of this had anything to do with them. They would make their move later when the time was right.

As yet, there was no sign of Cleave but I had the notion that he was close. I needed him. Much of Cleave's life had faded away without him even being aware of it, but he would be here when I needed him most. Of that, I had no doubt.

'I think you should stay with your friends, Brinkley,' I said. 'Being shot now is a little better than being hung later. Leastways it's quicker.'

'I don't know what you are talking about, boy.'

'I'm talking about a man who sets himself up as a wagon master so he can lead it into an ambush. Your friends followed this train all the way from Missouri. You spent some time away last night. You made your report to Dexter, warned him again that Cleave and Cole were the ones to watch out for. Don't reckon I earned a mention. That was just one of your mistakes. You're a damned fool; we were with you all the way.'

'You're a liar, boy,' Brinkley exploded, glancing at Dexter and not liking the set of his jaw. If he had slipped up Dexter would extract a heavy penalty.

'Nobody followed me. I back-tracked a few

times to make sure. I don't make mistakes like that.'

'Nope,' Dexter said, watching my grin widen. 'Your mistakes are a lot bigger than that. You just confessed to being part of my outfit. The kid's right, Brinkley: you are a damned fool. We can't afford people like you.'

Brinkley knew what that meant. The sentence of death had been passed. Dexter had already dismissed him. His full attention was back on me again. 'Well, now you got us, kid, what are you going to do with us? The odds are pretty much against you. You can't expect much help from a bunch of farmers. They are more likely to shoot each other. Close up like this, it would be hard to tell whose side they're on. You're on your own, boy.'

His logic penetrated the minds of the men moving to their wagons to pick up their weapons. Most of them came to a halt, and Blaine looked at me for instructions.

'He called it, Mister Blaine,' I said. 'Best if you all stayed out of it. It's down to us.'

'Us, kid?' Dexter questioned. 'All I see is you.'

'I'm not dumb enough or greedy enough to take on seven men,' I said easily. 'I'm not forgetting about Brinkley's two friends.'

'You can now,' Cole said, striding out into the centre of the wagon circle. 'They've been took care of.'

146

'That's Cole Masters,' I told Dexter. 'Don't reckon Cleave Devlin is too far away.'

'Not far,' Cleave agreed from the shadow of a nearby wagon. 'You picked your targets, Jim?'

'Brinkley and Squint there. Don't reckon I'll sleep easy until I put lead into them.'

'Good. Dexter's mine. It's long overdue.'

Dexter's eyes searched to penetrate the deep shadows of the wagon but failed. Some of the colour and confidence had faded from him. 'Seems to me I've heard that voice before,' he said quietly.

'You have, a long time ago. I should have killed you then. It's your choice, Dexter: a bullet now or a rope tomorrow.'

'Not much of a choice, is it?' Dexter asked, his brain still striving to identify the voice. 'Who taught the kid to use a gun? You?'

'Nope. Cole Masters did. But it's the next best thing,' Cleave answered. 'You always were one to figure out the odds. They're not good, Dex.'

'The least you can do is show me who I'll be shooting at,' Dexter said. 'I know the voice but I never heard the name Cleave Devlin until a few weeks back. Maybe you've got something to hide, too. You afraid to show your face Mister Devlin?'

'He's fine where he is,' Cole said, a sense of urgency in his tone. All along I had had the feeling that Cole was hiding something from me; some kind of secret he shared only with Cleave, and I wasn't allowed to be a part of it. Even now I could feel the fear in him. He was trying to protect Cleave, but I didn't know why.

'Now is as good a time as any,' Cleave answered, a weariness clouding his voice. 'I'm tired of living in the shadows. A lie can only stretch so far before it snaps back on a man. It's time he found out about me.'

'He isn't ready yet. He can't handle it.'

'We've still got a long way to go, Cole, and each day that lie is stretching further. It's time we tested his mettle. We are going to need him.'

Whatever they were talking about, I had the feeling that I wouldn't like it. But I was about to find out. Cleave was stepping out of the shadows.

Fourteen

The breath caught in Dexter's throat as Cleave stepped out of the shadows. The odds had suddenly switched against them.

'You're missing something since I seen you last. If I had known about the arm I might have put two and two together. Doubt it though. I had heard you were dead.'

'As good as,' Cleave said quietly. 'Maybe it would have been better if I had died. No guilt in death. Any time you feel like making your move, go ahead. It's a long time since I pulled iron against a man. Could be I've slowed up without even knowing it.'

Any other time I would have been unable to take my eyes off them, but I had Squint and Brinkley to keep in mind. Dexter was already dying when Squint made his move, gambling that my attention would be on Cleave and Dexter. He was wrong. My bullet took him square in the chest, lifting him off his feet. Brinkley died a second later. In the space of a couple of minutes five men lay dead or dying on the ground. I cursed myself for not feeling guilt at Brinkley and Squint's death. This isn't the way it should be. A man should always feel remorse at the taking of a life.

At least, Cleave had the right feelings in him as he stood over Dexter, watching his life ebb away. Blood flecked his lips as he spoke. 'Brinkley was a damned fool. He never learned how to read men. He should have known about the kid, too. Masters must be a good teacher. Cully was no slouch with a gun.'

His eyes sought me out through the haze of pain. I was starting to feel the way I had when the young Ute died. It wasn't my bullet that was killing Dexter but I was responsible for other deaths here tonight. I had set off on this trail with an urge to kill, but never realized I would feel this way as I watched a man's life fade away. This man was a stranger, a man needed to die because of his crimes. But my crime when I killed Jefferson Wilde would be the most terrible crime of all.

I was beginning to hope that I would never meet up with Jefferson Wilde.

Dexter's fist tightened as he fought against the pain. 'You got a name, boy? I'd like to know.'

'Jim Wilde,' I told him gently.

The easy smile replaced the snarl on his face. 'Should have known. You played us like fish on a line. It's the kind of thing Jeff would have done. I was up against a stacked deck all the time and didn't even know it. Only good thing about dying, kid, is it gets done but once.'

His body stiffened as life ebbed from his eyes. 'See you in hell, Jeff,' he said and died.

'Might be sooner than you think, Dex,' Cleave answered, looking at me. 'Depends upon just how good a teacher Cole is.'

Finally I knew what Cleave and Cole double-talk had been about all along. I felt sick and empty inside. They had been playing games with me all the way, keeping their secret safe and laughing behind my back. The man I was searching for was right at my side, and I hadn't even suspected a thing. Damn it. Wasn't there anyone in the world I could trust?

A tremor of shock ran through my body as I tried to unscramble my senses. Maybe it was a mistake. I had just misheard Dexter's last words. There was no real memory of Jefferson Wilde in me, just a vague picture of a tall man working around the farm with very little time to spend with me. Once in a while he had held me, but I had felt no real affection. Jeff Wilde hadn't been a man to show any emotions or feelings. Maybe they were locked so tight inside him that he couldn't

151

release them. Cleave Devlin had seemed somehow different to the man I remembered.

Cleave was a man who knew emotions, understood them, and wasn't shamed by them. He knew his own weaknesses and fought against them. Both the bottle and morphine addiction had been beaten by him. But this was one fight he couldn't hope to win.

I could see the truth in his eyes then as he faced me; his hands loose and ready near his gunbutt. 'It's your decision now, Jim. Nothing I say will change your mind about me. But whatever you decide, remember you've got to live with it after.'

If there was one thing I had learned from farm work it was patience, but it was running out on me now. Finding and killing Jefferson Wilde had been the only focus in my life for as long back as I cared to remember. He had to pay for all the suffering he had caused Ma and me.

'You've proved yourself with a gun too many times, Mister Wilde,' I told him tight-lipped, 'but there ain't enough bullets in that gun of yours to stop me killing you before I die.'

'Dying isn't hard, Jim,' he said quietly. 'Anyone can do it. Living is the hard part, and getting it right. I've got a second chance at it. I promised these folks that I'd get them safely to Oregon, and I can't let you break my word to them. It took me a long time to come face to face with myself. I still

152

don't like what I see but I'm getting there.'

The gunshot interrupted us, and we both turned to see the ashen face of Eli Mobley looking down at the twitching body of Ike Sims. Shock mirrored in his face and his voice trembled when he spoke. 'He had a pistol in his hand. He was going to kill someone. I ... I couldn't let him do that. I had to stop him.'

Suddenly realizing that the rifle was still in his hands, he tossed it away in disgust. Tears filled his eyes. 'I ... I had to stop him. There was no one else around. God...'

Eli Mobley was one of the kindest gentlest men I had ever known. His whole life revolved around his wife and family, and I doubt that he had ever had a bad thought about another human being in his life. He had stopped his wagon last week and went in search of a young injured cottontail he had spotted. The rabbit now lived happily in the back of his wagon as part of his family. And there would be no complaints from Mobley when the rabbit helped itself to his crop when he got his farm established in Oregon. It was an accepted part of life, and each tiny creature had its role to play. There were too few men like Eli Mobley in this world.

It felt like the ultimate intrusion just standing there watching a man die. A gun barked again and Sims died suddenly, Cleave's bullet buried deep in his heart. For the first time I could really accept Cleave as the man I had hated for so many years. This was his true self – Jefferson Wilde, natural born killer, a man without feelings. The hate was bubbling inside me like lava seeking its way to the surface as I watched him put the gun back into leather.

'Why? There was no need. The man was already—'

'The man was nothing, boy,' he interrupted me. 'Nothing. We would have wasted a lot of time waiting for him to recover, and then I would have had to put a rope around his neck. We can't afford that time. Doesn't matter much if I kill him with a rope or a gun, does it?'

'It wouldn't matter to you,' I snapped. 'It will never matter to you how you murder a man, will it?'

Something akin to pain touched his face, but didn't last. 'It's done now, boy. I just killed him and that's it. Plenty of witnesses to that fact.' He glanced at Cole. 'You were right – he isn't ready yet.'

He walked away then without a backward glance at any of us. Cleave Devlin – Jefferson Wilde. Were they one and the same or two different men, each a stranger to the other? I didn't know. Probably never would. Either way I would have to hold on to my hate until we reached

Oregon. My need to kill him was stronger than ever, but these people's need for him to lead them to Oregon was greater than my personal feelings. I could wait.

Cole Masters' cold eyes rested on me for a long time before glancing at the departing figure of Cleave Devlin, or whoever he was now. He had set his trap and I had blindly walked into it. Cleave and he had been laughing behind my back ever since the first day we had met.

'Well, you had your chance, kid. You've waited a long time to face up to Jeff Wilde. How come you didn't kill him? That's all you're living for, isn't it?'

'There are other people involved,' I told him. 'They want to get to Oregon. When the time is right I'll keep my word, but I'll make sure you're in front of me too when that time comes. You've been stabbing me in the back ever since I've known you. Not much difference between that and shooting a man in the back, is there?'

I walked away, leaving him to ponder my words. Doubted that he'd feel any guilt though. Cole Master's first and only loyalty was to the man now calling himself Cleave Devlin. Maybe, just maybe, I was feeling a touch of jealousy, too. There was a bond between the two men that I had never shared with the man who had once called me son.

Scooping the pup up into my arms after I had saddled the sorrel I rode off into the dark night, feeling the need to get away from people. A light rain was falling and the pup snuggled under my slicker to avoid it, but I didn't mind the rain. Back home, we had seen too little of it. I wished I was back there now. At least there I knew most of the problems I would be faced with and how to handle them.

Out here, each day brought a new worry, one I wasn't able to cope with. Jefferson Wilde should have remained just a shadow in my past. The real thing was someone I couldn't understand or deal with. A thousand questions assaulted my brain and I had no answers. Cleave Devlin was a man I had grown to know and like yet tonight, against everything I had believed about him, he had murdered a man without cause or reason. Sims was already dying so why was it so important that Jeff Wilde's bullet be the one that killed him?'

There was no sense to it. He hadn't made himself any new friends tonight. Even those that already knew and trusted him had looked with horror at his action. Damn, he was no better than the rawhiders. This wasn't the man Ma had spoken about with such love and tenderness. She had lived her life in the firm belief that one day Jefferson Wilde would reappear on the horizon and life would be good again.

She was wrong, but Ma had always been one to look for the good in people, tried to teach me the same way. Maybe it was a blessing that she hadn't lived to see what the man she loved had become.

Daybreak found me at rest in a stand of timber, looking back the way we had come. Movement in the distance caught my eye, and I reached for the field glasses in my saddle-bags. More Indians? More trouble? Four men came into sight, a fifth lagging behind. Five tired, worn out men with no longer any taste for pursuit. Kelp hadn't given up, after all. I headed back for the wagon train.

They were watering the horses at a creek when I rode up. I could feel the sudden tension in the air when I hove into sight. Only Lindy seemed relieved to see me, but I could read doubt in her eyes as I dismounted, letting Dancer wander to the creek. Eli Mobley moved away from Cleave Devlin's side – I still found it hard to think of him as the man I had set out to kill – as I moved towards them. Strange that. I would have thought that Devlin was the last man he would have wanted to spend time with. The look of horror froze on his face as I approached.

Eli was a man born to violent times but would never learn to live with violence. It was alien to his whole being, yet why should he have chosen to spend time in the company of the likes of Jefferson Wilde?

I knew the answer to that then. I had been too blinded by hate to even look for the truth about Jeff

Wilde. He and Cleave Devlin were one and the same man, and I was proud to know both. Sims had had to die under Jeff Wilde's gun because Eli Mobley could never learn to live with the knowledge that he had taken another man's life.

Cole Masters moved between me and Cleave, his hand near his gunbutt. 'Guess it's time to find out how well I taught you, kid.'

'Kelp and his bunch are heading this way,' I said quietly. 'About two hours behind us, I'd say.'

'We'll handle them when they come,' Cole said. 'He's not your fight. You led him to Jeff with a little help from me. That's all he ever wanted.'

'Still wet-nursing him, huh, Cole? Thought he'd be big enough to take care of his own problems by now. Time you found yourself a new life.'

I raised my right hand to adjust my hat. 'Looked to me like Kelp's lost his taste for a fight. Wouldn't take much to discourage him. A show of force would send him back the way he came from.'

'Always was that way with Kelp, needed a lot of back-up. Why are you telling us all this, kid?'

'Because I reckon it's time you found some new kind of employment. Nurse-maiding ain't no fit job for a grown man. I can see how you've been feeling sorry for him all those years. He ain't much but bringing him along with us could be the making of him. Know it's helped me. I can see things more clearly now.'

A slow grin started to spread along Cole Masters' face. 'Looks like Kelp is coming into more trouble than he can handle, kid. Got somebody in mind for my nurse-maid's job?'

'Seems like it's down to me. Like I said: he ain't much, but he's the only kin I've got.'